Andrew Roby

DOUBLE VISION

A creative crime drama

tredition®

© 2019 Andrée Roby

Cover, Illustrations: Micaela Grove

Editing: Régine Demuynck

Publisher: tredition

ISBN

Paperback　ISBN 978-3-7482-2126-5

Hardcover　ISBN 978-3-7482-2127-2

eBook　　　ISBN 978-3-7482-2128-9

All rights reserved

ACKNOWLEDGEMENTS

This book is dedicated to my father André Demuynck and to my favorite uncle Marcel Roby. It is the fruit of a brainstorming session one October evening with Micaela, my daughter, and her partner Jaco. I loved this incredible adventure of writing a book, so thank you so much for believing in my dream and for pushing me to go for it.

Heartfelt thanks to Sue, Maureen, Adrienne, Debbie, Micaela and Andy who were willing to read my words at various stages, to encourage me and challenge me all the way. They all helped shape this story.

Extra thanks to Sue for suggesting the title and for the hours she spent proofreading.

Thank you to my talented daughter who designed the book cover. I am very proud to have her work being the face of my story.

Thank you to my husband, my doggy and my cat for their patience when I was so engrossed in writing that I almost forgot they existed…

INTRODUCTION

As she was getting ready to go on her date, sheer excitement warmed her body in a way never experienced before. Her pulse was racing, her hands were trembling as she applied her make-up, little bubbles of laughter kept popping in her throat and, by the feel of it, her stomach was doing somersaults; all these amazing sensations at the thought of meeting him, this Adonis she had fancied for some time. Well, in less than an hour she would be with him.

In fact, she had felt brave booking him for the night. She longed for love, romance, sex, the full Monty really Why shouldn't she? Why would she not have it all? Who had thrown the dice of her particular life and decided she should not be loved the way she deserved and wanted? Who knows? The thought that she was middle-aged and had never been loved sounded pathetic even to her own ears.

In her innocence, she thought loving, wandering hands would make her body come to life, make her feel all woman. She yearned to be hugged, to let herself wallow in love, to share her life, in mind, body and soul.

It would have been feasible all those years ago, had her life not been plagued by the anger inside of her. She felt she had spent her life fighting against it. The more she fought it, the worse it got, as if her inner conflict was the perfect fuel to keep the fire burning. She knew it consumed her, in every fibre of her being. Her anger burned red hot in her heart, mind and soul.

True, nothing good would happen in her life until she silenced the volleys of angry arguments and insults which often erupted in her head like a volcano, targeting anyone who had ever slighted her. Arguments so damaging and intense, her limbs would go numb and her heart heavy, as if her blood only sustained the red hot anger and no longer her body. Anger so rampant inside that she felt herself tensing, ready to pounce on anybody who happened to be nearby.

Right at this point, anything might tip her over, making her lose her sanity and all notion of right or wrong. She felt like lashing out, kicking, hitting, and at worst, maiming someone to death.

She had been warned many times to stay out of trouble and, without a doubt, that was her intention tonight…

CHAPTER 1

Vince was what you would call a handsome young man with a sunny personality but rather immature for his 23 years of age. Popular with the ladies, charming when needed, able to tell a good joke, yet not afraid of showing his vulnerable side.

Neither ambitious nor educated, he had left school at 16 to work at McDonald's, then held a variety of low paid jobs up to two years ago. All in all, not a successful man by today's standard. But Vince considered himself a good man and an honest man. The one good thing going for him, really, was his physique on which he had worked for a few years, going to the gym several times a week, working with weights to increase the bulging muscles on his arms and legs.

At 18, he had indulged his childish, irresponsible streak by buying a motorbike which he dubbed his "bird-pulling" machine. Despite his pitiful wages, Vince had saved some money, allowing him to fork out £5,000 for a long-desired second-hand Harley. His greatest pleasure was to ride it down the streets of his native South London town, where women would invariably stare at him.

He would travel up to London whenever he fancied, extending his hunting ground. Vince was so obsessed by his bike that he would ride it regardless of the unpredictable British weather.

Flaunting all safety regulations, Vince liked nothing better than to ride his Harley without a helmet so that his unusual, beautiful red shoulder-length hair would float in the air, attracting attention from passers-by. He knew it was illegal, as well as not practical as his hair flew in his face, but Vince loved the fact that most women he came across were glancing at him appreciatively or even with lustful stares sometimes. When he liked the appearance of a particular woman, he would slow down to give them both a chance to appraise each other. He thrived on the stares and attention he was getting.

However, it did bother him a bit that sometimes men also studied him with interest and even with lust in their eyes but "heh! Live and let live" he would think. He was a ladies' man and men had never been, and never will be, his thing, but he was powerless to stop them staring at him.

Two and a half years ago, a lucky break came his way and he started working as a barman in a nightclub. The good years thus began....

Because of his red hair, club-goers (mainly women) would always strike up a conversation with him, asking if the colour was real etc. He had been born in a family of Irish descent who all possessed magnificent red manes just like his. His grand-parents and his mother all sported a head of flaming red hair.

He had realised that women favoured straight shoulder-length hair and that style framed his oval face very well. He also had piercing green eyes that he had learnt to use to connect with women's nurturing side. He was fond of using what he called his "puppy dog eyes", gazing straight at them, head tilted to the side, with childish puzzlement on his handsome face.

This was a seduction tactic he perfected when he first worked in the club two years ago as a means to get women to think he was a bit lost, a bit vulnerable and that, like a dog, he would be so grateful if they took care of him. And so started his new career as a gigolo (or as a male escort to be politically correct).

Well who would have thought? HIM! Vince O'Shaunessy!

Making a living by escorting single, lonely women to shows, art galleries, restaurants etc. and quite often offering extra "night-time" services! When he had first started his escort job, he had carried on working at the club which provided him with a good supply of eager clients, but he became so busy and tired that he had to resign.

Still it had served its purpose and he was now an established male escort.

Life was good for Vince. He had bought his own place in a leafy little street of Anerley with the added bonus of his own parking space for his cherished bike, no longer fearing that it would get damaged or stolen when left on the road. At the very beginning, he had gone out with women just to get a free meal, to spend an evening in someone's company and sometimes to get laid. But as he became popular, he decided to make his hair, his body and his handsome face work for him.

For two years now he had been paid to eat with women in trendy places, to go to fashionable places and, above all, to have sex with them and this suited him well. He certainly did not know many people who, like him, were getting paid very well to eat, go out, have fun and get laid!

During that period, there had been a few young women whom he had found attractive enough to have become attached to, had he not kept to his goal of earning as much as possible, for as long as possible - and certainly he envisaged doing this "job" until he was at least 40 years old.

His reputation as a male escort had grown this last year, as word of mouth was providing him with more and more ladies of any age and background, eager to avail themselves of his services. Many of them were professional women who were career-focussed and did not have time to date, but still enjoyed going out with an attractive, interesting man and spending a very pleasant evening.

Most of the women who contacted him did so by phone. One evening he took a call from a lady called Vanessa, whom he had never heard from before. She requested his company for an impromptu alternative art exhibition at the Dulwich Picture Gallery, then dinner also in Dulwich afterwards. Arrangements were made to meet one Thursday night at the end of October. He gave her a description of himself and instructions as to where he would wait for her.

When he met her at the agreed time outside the Dulwich Picture Gallery, Vince was a little surprised by the blonde woman who had requested his services. Not exactly attractive, tall but not over-tall, a bit heavy, with slightly angular features on a longish face. Her smoky voice when she introduced herself reminded him of a late-night radio presenter.

"Hum, unusual woman!" he concluded.

Her hair was blonde and styled in a long bob. He guessed she might be in her late 40s. Because of the make-up she wore, it was challenging to give her a definite age. Somehow he was feeling a bit uneasy about her. The reason for the uneasiness eluded him but he was convinced that something was not quite right. Not willing to lose the £500 (or more) that he would earn escorting Vanessa tonight, he decided to put his uneasiness at the back of his mind and to concentrate on what Vanessa was saying.

Very early on in his new career, Vince had realised that being a good listener was a key skill to ensuring his success, followed by being knowledgeable about a variety of subjects so that conversation flowed during his meetings with clients. Skills all the more important, as he lacked academic qualifications.

Going around the exhibition, Vanessa revealed herself to be an interesting companion, knowledgeable about art, current affairs and most probably gastronomy. She had chosen a gourmet restaurant in Dulwich near the Picture Gallery. When booking him for the evening, she had made it clear that she wanted the extra "night-time services" he offered. Vince had duly booked a room at the four star hotel he favoured in Forest Hill, the Woodman Inn.

The weather that evening was quite mild and dry for an October evening so they agreed to walk the short distance from the restaurant to the hotel. Walking alongside Vanessa towards it, Vince was asking himself why her voice was a bit strained. Thinking she was maybe feeling a little nervous and uncomfortable herself, he made small talk to alleviate her concerns.

On arrival at the Woodman Inn, Vince picked up the key to their room from reception. On the way in, he had slipped a generous tip to the concierge who would ensure that a taxi would be waiting for the client when she left the hotel in the morning. He always made a point of leaving before sunrise and letting the lady have the room to herself until the morning.

A rule, he had set himself from the beginning which gave him a failsafe if necessary. He also always organised for room service to bring breakfast to the lady, so he had asked Vanessa at what time it should be brought to her. Whenever possible, he left his bike at the hotel, then made his way to meet his date either on foot, by taxi or by tube depending on where their meeting took him. This way he just left when he wanted.

They took the lift to the 5th floor in silence. This part of the evening often filled him with apprehension.

What would she be like naked and in bed? Would he be able to perform? Would she have strange requests or be so boring that he would not be able to rise to the occasion? Well there was no point wondering anymore as they had reached the 5th floor and were now walking towards room 505.

CHAPTER 2

Vanessa was enjoying her evening and her companion. She had noticed him many times before tonight, at the club where he used to work, or recklessly riding his bike in the streets of Anerley, with his distinctive red hair floating in the wind. She had often thought that it was lucky he had not been stopped by the police whilst riding without a helmet so many times. He always appeared so carefree. She had taken a fancy to him. She would have loved to ride with him on his flashy bike and to feel his gorgeous hair floating in her face.

On a visit to the club a year ago, she had even managed to take a picture of him. She had pretended to take a selfie whilst he was standing behind the bar. Of course, he had not even noticed her so he was unlikely to realise that she had taken a picture of him. Then, during subsequent visits, she had noticed his repeated absence so she had asked the manager about him. She had been both surprised and delighted to learn that he was now a full-time male escort. What a stroke of luck! She was realistic enough to know that she would never be able to attract the attention of such a handsome, much younger, man by herself.

In truth she had very little chance of going out with him for an evening unless she paid for his services.

Vanessa knew that, in the looks department, she had been somewhat short-changed. She was tall but a bit stocky. Her voice, a touch irritating to some people, was husky most of the times. When asked about it, she would blame it on having smoked since her teens. She told them that she had now stopped but the huskiness in her voice had remained. She thought her face was slim and interesting, though not pretty. Shame that she tended to be a bit heavy handed with her make-up. She had never taken the time to learn how to apply it properly but it did not bother her. Her hair tonight was blonde but it was not always that colour. Vanessa had assumed that blondes were more likely to be Vince's type.

As a result of her less than pleasing appearance, by the age of 45, she had never married. No-one had ever taken enough interest in her to offer a long-term relationship or marriage. She was considered too aloof and too much of a loner. In truth, relationships had been a major issue since puberty - not only did she lack self-confidence but she had an almost pathological fear of rejection.

This fear, she knew, stemmed from being bullied repeatedly throughout her schooling resulting in deep emotional scars. She had been breathing shame and guilt every minute of her time spent at secondary school.

Vanessa had never felt that she "fitted in" with the other kids at primary school, then at secondary school and even later on at university. She was always dubbed "a freak" because of the way she dressed, and because she just did not relate to people well. Being so uncomfortable in her own skin made her a magnet for loud-mouthed bullies who enjoyed tormenting her for years. The regular taunts of "freak, weirdo, and sicko" were still resounding aloud in her head all those years later.

She had learnt to silence the voices but, on occasions, the memories resurfaced and that would make her angry with the bullies, and sometimes with herself, for not standing up to them. She often felt like a volcano ready to erupt at any moment.

She had not been lucky either in her professional life and had not achieved what she had dreamt of doing as a young person. Work was not fulfilling and had proved to be a big disappointment a few months back.

But tonight, walking on the arm of handsome Vince, through the exhibition at the Dulwich

Picture Gallery, and then sitting in a trendy restaurant talking to him during the meal, she was feeling happy. Of course she chose to ignore the fact that his charming presence was costing her a hefty £500. She even had had the courage to tell him that she wanted some of the other services he provided, the one he gallantly called the extra "night-time services".

Vince took her to a hotel, the Woodman Inn. She waited for him whilst he spoke to the concierge. He had told her that he would organise a taxi for her to get home in the morning as he would be leaving during the night. She was not pleased with the prospect of waking up alone. She did that every morning. By paying for his services she had expected a long, romantic, sex filled night… Well at least, she would get breakfast in the room at eight o'clock, small consolation in her opinion.

She swallowed her disappointment, something she had become better and better at doing over the years, and followed him into the lift, up to the 5th floor and along the corridor to room 505.

Vince, always a gentleman, opened the door to a bright and modern room, let Vanessa in, and took her coat off for her.

As requested, a bottle of champagne left by the maid was chilling in an ice-bucket on the small desk opposite the bed. Vince offered her a glass which she drank with anticipation.

In all honesty, she hoped the champagne would give her some Dutch courage. Paying for a male escort and for sexual services was a new experience. She had felt very brave to have contacted him but, as the moment she had dreamt of for so long was approaching, she was feeling both scared and excited.

Vince came closer and gently kissed her. So far this evening there had been no physical contact apart from holding his arm in the art gallery, and him helping her to take off, and put on, her coat at the restaurant. Vanessa, a bit of a traditional sort, thought that Vince was the perfect gentleman so she was enchanted by him. She had fancied him for so long that, at last to be on the verge of having sex with him, gave her butterflies in her stomach.

She wondered if he felt anything towards her in the way she did towards him, but she put that thought out of her mind. No point asking for the moon. She would not get a boyfriend from this encounter, but at least she will be having sex with a handsome younger man.

The memory of their sexual encounter might keep her warm during lonely nights ahead. Uneventful, lonely, cold nights had been her lot every night forever.

She was not a virgin as such, but that shameful and traumatic encounter with a fellow university student 25 years ago, did not qualify her as being sexually knowledgeable. That was an experience she had not wanted to repeat. But, tonight, she had high hopes for something magical with handsome Vince.

"Let's face it, for £500 I expect fireworks and all the trimmings". She almost laughed to herself.

After the champagne and the gentle kisses, Vince took Vanessa in his arms and kissed her with apparent fervour. He had no romantic thoughts towards her, rather he was thinking instead that it was midnight already, and he needed to get on with the job in order to leave at three am as planned. He had become very skilful in the art of pretending feeling romantic and of being excited by his client, so Vanessa did not notice that he was somewhat distracted.

She was enjoying herself and waited impatiently for their sexual encounter although her apprehension level was high. The unfortunate sexual experience of years ago was foremost in her mind.

Vince led her to the bed and laid down next to her, fully clothed for now. He was starting to undress her, he unbuttoned her blouse very slowly, kissing her neck at the same time and she eagerly returned his kisses. Once the blouse was undone, Vince was about to undo her bra when Vanessa gently pushed him away.

"Sorry, I would prefer to keep my bra on. I feel a bit embarrassed". Vanessa's voice was a coarse whisper. "I am afraid that I have had a double mastectomy and I am waiting for reconstructive surgery, so for now I am using prosthetics".

Vince's eyes narrowed and he examined her with a mixture of compassion and understanding but also confusion. With her clothes on, she had appeared to have a reasonable-size chest and he would never have guessed her breasts had not been real.

"Of course, no problem. Sorry to hear that". Vince moved his hands away from her bra fastening and started to unzip her skirt.

The feeling of uneasiness, which he had experienced when he first met her, reappeared and he wondered what it was about Vanessa that made him uneasy. Had he sensed that she was not a "complete" woman? This was absurd, as he had no way of guessing what she had just explained to him.

Vanessa had moved towards him and was kissing him whilst pulling him to her urgently. He disengaged himself from her embrace, stood near the bed and undressed, removing first his shirt, exposing a well-defined torso. Next his trousers came off, revealing strong thighs and long legs as well as smart blue Calvin Klein underwear. In a quick gesture, he removed his underwear. All the while, her lustful stare had been locked onto his body, and now that he was naked, onto his, not so private, parts. Never in his career had he felt so uneasy about being naked in front of a client. What was going on with him? He was finding it difficult to conjure up an erection which would prove to her that he was as eager to make love as she was.

Vanessa got off the bed to let Vince remove her skirt, then stood a few paces away from him, in her bra and tights. She lowered her gaze, almost sheepishly.

Misunderstanding her emotions, Vince thought she was scared or embarrassed, so he gently pulled her to him, held her tight in his arms to soothe her anxiety.

Whilst pressed against her, Vince was overcome by an almighty realisation that he knew what had made him uneasy. For there, staring down at her genitals, was a clear bulge, albeit squeezed compactly inside the tights and tight underwear, which was not at all feminine.

Vince's eyes widened at the unexpected sight and he pushed her away from him, recoiling in horror:

"What the hell? You're a bloke! Why the fuck didn't you tell me, you freak! You are sick, pretending to be a woman. Why didn't you warn me? Did you expect to fuck me or that I would give you a blow job or something?? You make me sick…"

By now Vince was furious, even shocked to find himself in this situation. He felt sick to his stomach and repulsed by this man pretending to be a woman, wanting HIM to make love to HIM. Never had this happened before! He had nothing against gay people or cross dressers, or transvestites for that matter, but it was not his inclination.

Vince, shaken, suddenly intensely nauseous, wanted out of this nightmare scenario. He bent down to gather his clothes. He was so agitated that he was struggling to pick them all up. He did his utmost to avert his gaze from her crotch area, thinking that it was all surreal.

"I am leaving. Do what you want but I have no intention of staying here with you. God almighty what a night!" he moaned, finally having gathered his clothes, staggering away from Vanessa to get dressed and leave the hotel as soon as possible.

CHAPTER 3

Vanessa, equally shocked, had stood rooted to the spot, all the while processing the fact that Vince was walking away from her, showing her his back, clutching at his clothes. This was not supposed to happen. She felt a brief, intense sadness at this new rejection. An unbearable pain seared her heart. An upsetting childhood memory crossed her mind.

It reminded her of her favourite ornament being destroyed by her dad with a hammer, tiny fragments of porcelain shattered on the table. At this very minute, her heart too was shattered to smithereens.

Then as quick as a bolt of lightning, the sadness gave way to a much stronger feeling. The anger was spreading its destroying fingers through her brain. The familiar thoughts now crowded her head; the relentless taunts of "freak", the traumatic memory of the unwelcome sodomisation suffered at the hands of a drunk fellow university student, the feelings of humiliation and de-gradation which had plagued her for months afterwards. All of it crystal clear in her mind.

In every cell of her body, she felt the anger, the humiliation, the isolation, the "not belonging", the need to sneak out dressed as a woman, the rejection by society and by men, of her, as a woman, the frustration of the lack of sexual intimacy, the lack of identity.

All these spiralling feelings drove her out of control. Finally the hot rage, the hot iron marks left on her heart, the hurtful words taunting her like a red rag to a bull, all erupted from her tormented mind, seeking revenge, intensifying the desire to hit out, to maim.

The intense repulsion she had witnessed on Vince's face, his body recoiling from her as if touched by something disgusting and repulsive, brought her to the tipping point. Her nostrils widened as they flared in and out and in that moment, she lost all rational thinking and jumped on Vince's back, seized him by the neck, forcing him down on the bed, unsure what to do next but unable to stop herself from inflicting harm.

The urge was too great, the force inside was gathering momentum, the need to inflict retribution to this man left her devoid of any humanity and compassion. Nothing would stop her now; her suffering had to be avenged once and for all; her rage was finding its voice at long last.

She had caught him by surprise so he lost his footing toppling down on the bed with Vanessa on top of him. He was as shell-shocked as she was enraged and his reflexes were too slow. He had no idea what was going on. He had wanted to leave and put this behind him but Vanessa's reaction stunned him. Violence had never featured in his life so the viciousness of her assault was bewildering him.

Right at this moment, the years of going to the gym and of body building paid off though. With unexpected strength, Vince managed to overthrow this tornado of rage and hysteria.

"Who the fuck is this woman? euh man? " he thought as cold shivers crept up his spine like an army of ants.

He ran to the bathroom, scared, confused, and dumbfounded by what was happening. Despite her stockiness, she sprang forward with surprising agility, following him closely, just as he reached for the shower curtain. He spun around, grabbed her in an arm-lock around her arms and chest with his left arm, all the while pulling on the shower curtain with his right hand. He yanked it down, pulling the rail down too.

Despite her attempts at freeing herself, Vince drew Vanessa tighter towards him and wrapped the curtain around her neck and chest, then toppled her over into the shower. Holding her down with his foot pressing on her back, he opened the cold tap, hoping that some cold water would calm her rage. He attempted to pacify her by pleading with her:

"Calm down, will you! We can talk about this. I am sorry I have offended you but you must admit that this is not usual   Come on, stop this, you are scaring me". Fear was imprinted on his face, like an ugly mask. His hands were flailing in front of him as if to shoo her away.

Clearly she was in a very angry mood; his words and reactions had had a far worse effect on her than he had imagined. She was demented, hysterical, vicious, all at the same time. The only sounds coming out of her mouth were animal-like grunts and sporadic angry words thrown at him. He did not even understand what she was grumbling, so intent was he to avoid more physical contact with her, wanting to remove himself from this crazy happening and leave the hotel as soon as possible. Right now, he was shit-scared of what she was going to do to him.

Managing to get out of the shower, wet but burning with hot rage, she wrenched the seat off the toilet with a strength he had not anticipated. She raised the seat over her head and brought it down repeatedly on his arms, his back, around his legs. He was moving backwards, away from her, all the while trying his best to prevent the forceful blows she was raining on him. Her strength was phenomenal. The blows all the more painful as he was devoid of the clothing which could have soften some of the impact.

"This is not happening". Baffled thoughts kept going around in Vince's mind. "This is not for real. Bloody hell, I'll wake up in a minute and it'll be fine".

His thoughts were going a hundred miles an hour in his head, his stomach was so tight and full of knots that he found it hard to breathe as he lunged towards the bedroom to escape further blows.

Rage propelled Vanessa further forward and she rugby-tackled Vince around the legs, just as he was nearing the bed. He fell face down on it. She was on top of him, on his back, in a flash.

Although stocky, and possibly as heavy as him, her main advantage was the searing hot rage which gave her an uncharacteristic physical strength.

She pressed on the small of his back with her right knee and raising herself slightly with her left leg on the bed, she grabbed Vince's left arm, yanked it up and back with such force she almost wrenched it out of its socket. Vince cried out in sheer agony as he tried to manoeuvre his body to face her, his mind befuddled, clouded by the pain.

Letting go of his arm, she used that opportunity to straddle him, grab a pillow and press it on his face with all her strength. Vince fought back, punching her body at random, trying to catch his breath to be able to fight her off. He was using his arms and legs, and twisting his body to shake her off him.

Eventually, by moving his head from side to side, he managed to loosen her grasp and get the pillow off his face. The air entered his lungs in a welcome rush. But just as he thought he had managed to overthrow her, she gave him an almighty kick in the balls. He lost his grip on her, his body twisting in more agonising pain.

In that instant, without hesitation, Vanessa put her hands around Vince's neck and squeezed withall her might, letting all the rage explode from her mind, heart and soul into her hands.

She had finally reacted after being called "a freak and a sicko" once too often.

She collapsed on top of him, trembling from the aftermath of her rage. His body below hers was motionless. Regardless, she held him in a romantic embrace. She pressed her lips on his lifeless face, then gently pulled a lock of his lovely red hair between her fingers, stroked it and smelled it. She had the sensation of being close to him now, her skin touching his, holding him in the loving way he had denied her a short while ago.

Right now, for the first time in her life, there was no rejection, he was all hers. She laid with him a little while longer. Her rage finally spent, reality sunk in. What had happened just then?

This man she had fancied for some time had been repulsed by her. She had not imagined that scenario when she had asked him to be her escort. In her naivety, she thought there might be some awkwardness but nothing like the tornado that had just struck them both.

The enormity of the situation hit her. She had killed a man! Driven by the poison inside her heart and mind, she had actually killed a man!

That thought gave her a jolt, like an electric discharge coursing through her.

She suddenly leapt away from his cold body, her nostrils all of a sudden aware of the smell of death surrounding him, feeling disgusted by his inert body, with his flaccid penis, nesting in pubic hair no woman will ever stroke again. He appeared almost indecent now. She was unable to bear the sight of Vince any longer.

Checking her watch, she realised that it was already one o'clock in the morning, so she had to get out of the hotel without arousing suspicion.

Vince's beloved bike, parked below in the hotel car park, was unlikely to be discovered until the morning. Still, she had to get out as quickly and as safely as possible. She knew that, when it came to it, the police would be searching for a woman.

A plan began to form in her h ead. She had to act quickly before rigor mortis started to set in. Maybe she had read too many detective stories, but she knew how to turn Vince's death into a sexual game of strangulation for plea-sure gone wrong.

She snatched a bathrobe from the bathroom, using the belt to tie Vince's arms above his head.

Then she placed the pillow over his deathly white, inert face again, oblivious of the now pathetic lock of red hair sticking out from under the pillow.

His body was laying on its back, naked, slightly twisted so the theory of a sexual game was plausible. She grabbed the bedding around him, crumpling it all into a ball which she threw on the floor, as if the lovers had been in a hurry to play unhampered and had stripped the bed.

Then she finally sat down to think clearly how to leave the hotel unnoticed.

CHAPTER 4

Ray Stevens had been in the police force since shortly after leaving university, first as a police officer then, somehow managing to pass the required tests, he had climbed to the position of Detective Inspector, which he had held for twenty years now. In his heart, though, he knew he was not very likely to ever make it to Detective Chief Inspector. One of his colleagues had just been promoted despite being in service for less years than Ray. That really rankled.

As a child, Ray had always wanted to be a carpenter but, changed his mind at the age of 16. Having watched a lot of detective series and films over the years, he decided that he wanted to be a policeman, preferably a detective. He felt that it was his duty somehow to help maintain the peace and to solve crimes. He also wanted to make something of himself after having failed to achieve good results throughout his schooling. He had not enjoyed school at all and, when his parents forced him to go to University, he was not pleased as the education system had been a nightmare for him. All he had wanted to do was to enter the police force at the age of 18 and skip university altogether.

But he complied with his parents' wishes and studied Criminal Justice and Policing as well as Forensic Science at Nottingham Trent University.

Now in his forties, Ray was unmarried and living alone in a small terraced house in a Gypsy Hill, a South London suburb, and was working in Croydon police station. He was not a handsome man but he was fairly tall. For some reason unknown to him, he had never been able to attract women. Clearly, there was something in his physique, or in his personality, they did not find attractive. He had always felt that he lacked the right social graces to please women. He felt extremely clumsy and shy around them. It didn't help that he was useless at making small talk. He liked conversation with a purpose so he never understood the necessity to just chit-chat with women or with anyone. That had not made him popular with either the opposite sex or with his work colleagues.

At times he felt a bit like he lived in a different world than the rest of humanity. Given all this, it was hardly surprising he had never met the right woman and, so far, had remained single.

Although, when he first joined the force as a police officer, in his early 20s, he had fancied a waitress who worked in a café across from the police station. He had tried his best for a few weeks to be sociable and pleasant but, eventually, had only managed to take her out one evening. He always thought of this episode with embarrassment for two reasons. Firstly, he remembered her as being a pretty girl with lovely eyes and beautiful hair that attracted him. It was just a bit unfortunate that "Margaret" was the name he had read on the badge on her waitress' uniform when he first met her. This was actually his grandmother's name!

Secondly, their very brief association had led nowhere. The waitress had refused to go out with him a second time. How humiliating it had been for Ray. Especially as all of his colleagues eating at the café had been aware of his attempts to seduce "Margaret".

After that debacle, over the years, he had had one night stands, usually whilst staying in a hotel to attend a police conference. He assumed that either the irony, or the kudos, of "screwing a policeman" was the attraction for some women to willingly have sex with him. He guessed that he had to be content with that. Though, from his point of view, it was not exactly a successful sex life.

At work, Ray was usually despatched to deal with RTAs (Road Traffic Accidents) when they appeared to be suspicious. What Ray lacked in social skills, he usually made up in investigating skills. He was a good detective, thorough, clear thinking, logical and open-minded. The only reason he was passed over for promotion was due to his lack of interaction with his colleagues, to the slightly gauche way in which he carried himself, making everyone think he was not comfortable in his own skin. That was true, he was not. Neither was he a good communicator.

One particular Friday morning in October, Detective Chief Inspector David Holroyd, called Ray in his office. There had been a bout of tummy bugs going around for a few days in the police station, and David Holroyd, Ray's superior, was sending him to a crime scene in a hotel in Forest Hill as three of his colleagues were off-sick with the virus.

Due to the extensive program of police station closures, detectives were being sent to investigate major incidents further and further afield. A sorry state of affairs which made Holroyd's job difficult when having to despatch some of his best detectives far from Croydon. Having officers who were ill was bad enough, without having to despatch the remaining officers to South London.

He gave Ray a quick outline of the case.

"A crime has been reported by the maid who went into room 505 at the Woodman Inn. She was bringing the guest breakfast at eight o'clock this morning. But then, when nobody answered she went in with her key. She discovered a man, on his own in the room, strangled, lying on the bed. She also mentioned that the young man has unusual red hair. For some reason she thought it might help us to identify him. Of course she is pretty shaken up. I have already sent a constable to secure the crime scene before you get there, Ray. Please go and keep me posted".

As ordered, Ray got in his car and drove to the Woodman Inn, where he was shown to the manager's office. He saw that the maid was still in shock, as was the concierge who had known the victim for a couple of years. He told Ray that Vince O'Shaunessy was a male escort who regularly used the hotel when his clients requested further services.

He explained that Vince always spoke to him on arrival to confirm the time for the lady's breakfast to be brought up and to secure a taxi for whatever time his client would choose to leave in the morning.

He added that Vince had a rule to never stay the whole night and he always left at the same time between three and three fifteen in the morning. He usually parked his bike in the hotel car park when he knew the client had requested "special services" so he was able to leave without any hassle. The concierge also confirmed that the bike was still in their car park.

Ray then enquired from the manager if there were CCTV cameras in the reception area, in the lift or in the corridors. Unfortunately the manager answered that the owner of the hotel had not been able to afford cameras on all floors and the one camera behind the reception desk, normally recording the comings and goings of guests, had been malfunctioning for a couple of days. An engineer was due in shortly to repair it. However, the concierge confirmed that Vince had been accompanied by a slightly older lady and gave a good description of her.

After taking statements from both the concierge and the maid, Ray made his way to the 5th floor, to room 505.

The constable despatched to the scene ahead of Ray was waiting for him in the doorway. Before entering the room, Ray instructed him:

"The concierge gave me the name of the victim, so call the office on your mobile to get someone to do a search on Vince O'Shaunessy, then ask an officer and a Family Liaison Officer to go and inform the next of kin. Ask them too to organise for the bike to be taken away for forensics".

Due to his poor communication skills, the painful task of informing families of the unfortunate fate met by one of their loved ones, was one Ray never relished doing. He found it challenging and harrowing at the same time. Throughout his life, he had always had to keep his emotions under control, so it was hard to witness the depth of grief displayed by a relative when informed that a loved one had passed away or even, as it was the case now, had been murdered. That was the part of the job he hated the most.

Inwardly bracing himself, Ray entered Room 505. The scene which greeted him was shocking, even for a seasoned detective.

The young man was sprawled naked on the unmade bed, lying on his back, his body twisted asin a final spasm, his arms tied above his head with a pillow placed on his face for good measure. Only a stray lock of his red hair was showing from under the pillow.

Ray donned some gloves and inspected the body more closely without disturbing its position. He was well aware that it was not be moved until the required pictures had been taken by the forensic photographer. On peering under the pillow, he noticed ugly deep red marks around the victim's neck. The man was obviously working out regularly in a gym as his muscled neck and body indicated, so it would take a strong person to strangle him. In his logical, analytical mind, Ray was already thinking that the murder was not down to a woman unless she had the physical strength needed to not only pin down such a young, fit man but to carry out a strangulation at the same time.

Back in the room after making the necessary phone calls, the constable next directed Ray to the bathroom which had been trashed as if a mad person had gone on the rampage, tearing the shower curtain from the railing and letting the water run in the shower which had partially flooded the room.

The toilet seat was missing. Judging by the broken fastenings on the floor, behind the toilet bowl, it had probably been yanked out. The constable voiced out loud what Ray was already thinking; that this was a challenging thing for a woman to do unless she was very strong. Or maybe really, really, angry.

A bathrobe sporting the hotel logo was still hanging on the bathroom door, untouched, but Ray noted that there was only one.

"The other one has obviously gone missing during the night", commented Ray to his colleague who noted this fact in his notebook.

In the room itself, there was an empty bottle of champagne and two glasses on the desk. The bed covers had been removed from the bed and were on the floor in a crumpled ball. At first glance, from the scene in the bedroom, maybe it was one of these weird sexual experiments he had heard of, where lovers use strangulation which is then released just at the point of orgasm. This, he had heard, was supposed to amplify the sexual pleasure experienced. However in this instance, the perpetrator had not stopped at the point of orgasm but had gone on to inflict death.

Well, Ray would have to wait for the coroner's findings after the post mortem is carried out. The man had probably been dead for a few hours but the time of death would be confirmed after further examination. Having studied Forensic Science, Ray took pleasure in setting himself a challenge.

When attending a crime scene, he would observe the purple markings on the body caused by livor mortis. This was a phenomenon less commonly known than rigor mortis, which occurred within a few hours of the death. The size of the markings appearing during livor mortis was an indication of how long the body had been dead, thus allowing the coroner to determine the exact time of death. Ray, inwardly of course, always congratulated himself for finding that, when guessing the time of death, he was usually accurate as confirmed later in the police report.

Small victory, he knew, but it made him feel clever and important. This was a skill he had perfected over the last ten years and he was proud of it.

From the state of the bathroom, the theory of sexual strangulation was not so probable. Rather, it pointed to something different and more sinister, like the pursuit of a victim by an assailant.

Earlier on, when examining the body closer, Ray had noted welts on Vince's arms, legs and buttocks congruent with being hit forcefully by a blunt object. The toilet seat had more than likely been used to hit Vince. However it was neither in the bedroom nor in the bathroom. Had the woman struck him to defend herself against Vince's advances or had he been the victim of a deranged, psychotic woman and if so, why kill him? If it was self-defence, why not contact the police? The fact that Vince's last client was nowhere to be found spoke volumes to his detective mind.

The team of crime scene investigators sent to take pictures, finger prints and lift off any other forensic evidence like DNA, had done their job whilst Ray and the constable were taking the statements and examining the room and the body.

There had been no finger prints or any other forensic evidence, which was not unusual but did not bode well for a speedy resolution of this murder investigation. There was no more to be gained by staying here so Ray signalled to the coroner's assistant to take the body away to the mortuary for the post mortem to be carried out.

The investigation into Vince O'Shaunessy's death would start in earnest. A murder investigation team would be put together quickly and, as he would most likely be part of it, there would be no weekend for him this week and probably no leave for weeks to come.

He did not mind. He knew that the first 48 hours after a murder were the most crucial in order to catch the perpetrator of the crime. The longer it took to find the culprit, the more likely this case would end up as an unsolved case (a cold case as it was known in the police force).

CHAPTER 5

Back at the police station, Ray handed over the statements to one of his colleagues to process and go through. He started searching for clues as to the identity of the female client by going through Vince's phone which had been found inside the crumpled bed clothes. He was glad the killer had forgotten to remove the phone as it may hold vital information about who had been with him that night. It was careless but very useful.

Unfortunately, it was proving impossible to trace the woman who had requested Vince's services. Having gone through the mobile phone carefully, Ray had himself checked all the numbers for dialled and received calls. Only one number was likely to correspond to his last client but it proved to be an unregistered number, probably a pay-as-you-go SIM card. The phone the woman had used must have been an old phone, or a very basic one, likely not GPS activated, as it was impossible to track down its owner or its current location. This was going to be a frustrating investigation!

John Clark, the officer in charge of informing the next of kin, came to tell Ray he had traced Vince's family by phoning the emergency number Ray had found in Vince's phone.

John had checked with the step dad, Jim, that Vince was indeed their son. Jim had been insistent that John Clark tell him why he was ringing so John informed him of Vince's death and that he was coming now to speak to him and to Vince's mother personally. John Clark was taking with him a family liaison officer whose role it was to help the entire family deal with this traumatic death.

Despite the numerous questions Vince's parents asked John Clark, the officer was not able to give them too much detail, only that he had been found naked and strangled in a hotel room where he had been with a woman for part of the night. He informed them that the woman was the prime suspect at this stage and they were doing their utmost to find out who and where she was. Jim and his wife were shattered by the news. John Clark informed them that the body would have to be formally identified to confirm that it was Vince. Jim volunteered to identify the body instead of his wife. He could not bear the thought of the distress it would cause her.

Vince had been like a son to him from the day he met his mother, so he wanted to spare her having to live with the memory of her murdered son's body lying on a slab in the mortuary!

John Clark further informed them that the body would not be released for some time as there would be a post mortem and the murder investigation was on-going.

Five minutes later, having dealt with one of the worst aspects of his otherwise enjoyable job, John Clark left the O'Shaunessy's home. The family liaison officer stayed behind to support them and assist them in anything they may need over the next few days. Both parents were torturing themselves with questions like "Why has Vince been murdered? What did he do to deserve this?" Both sincerely hoped for answers pretty soon.

Back at the police station, the investigation team was working diligently to find clues as to the identity of the suspected killer. The tickets for the Dulwich Picture Gallery exhibition, and a receipt for a meal at a Dulwich restaurant, dated the night of the murder, had been found in Vince's wallet. Ray was pondering why the murderer had so carelessly left behind some vital pieces of evidence like the wallet and the phone. Whoever it was must be pretty sure of not being caught.

Forensic had confirmed that no fingerprints had been found at the scene, none on the champagne glasses, none on the bed, none in the bathroom.

Nothing! The murderer had wiped them all.... Sexual penetration had not taken place as there was no trace of DNA either around Vince's groin area. Strange sexual game without the sex!!

Equally, the bike showed nothing other than Vince's fingerprints. The forensics team had drawn a blank.

The interviews and statements from staff at the Dulwich Picture Gallery, at the restaurant and at the hotel gave the picture of a woman, mid-to late 40s, with heavy make-up, blonde, fairly tall and stocky. The concierge thought that he had heard Vince call her Vanessa, but was not completely sure. The name Vanessa and her description were inputted into the central computer in case any information was held on her in the police database but nothing came up.

A search of Vince's apartment had provided a list of clients for the last two years but Vanessa was not on it. Of course, he had been murdered on their first date, so her name and contact details had not yet been entered in his book!

The manager of the night club was distraught to hear the news of Vince's demise but had no further information either about the mysterious Vanessa, if indeed that was the correct name.

Talk about a needle in a haystack. How many Vanessas were out having fun in London on that particular Thursday night?

For all they knew, she may not even be from London, or even from England.

The lack of progress was bothering Detective Chief Inspector David Holroyd. He had attended several briefings from the team and he knew that they had very little to go on. There was not enough physical evidence beyond Vince's body, his injuries and his phone, to link anyone to the crime yet and the woman was proving very elusive indeed. Without concrete evidence this case would not even go to the Crown Prosecution Services as it would be dismissed from the off. The investigation was at a standstill and desperately needed new leads to catch the killer.

Whilst attending a recent police conference, David Holroyd had been made aware by another Chief Inspector, that a vicious murder had been solved last year, after being stagnant for some time, thanks to the insight of a psychic clairvoyant. His colleague explained that a photo of the victim (a young girl) had been given to the psychic and she had come up with valuable information leading to the murderer's arrest.

All this information was coming back to David, especially given that the media had broadcasted the story for some days due to the identity of the victim and the unusual circumstances following her murder. His counterpart had even handed him one of the psychic young woman's business cards, should he ever need it. When he found her card, he would get Ray to contact her. She might be able to shed some light on the murderer.

It was an unusual step to take but some unusual crimes sometimes required unusual solutions. David Holroyd had never ruled out that some people had powers of intuition to perceive the events which took place enabling that person to help a case that was stalling. He vaguely recalled that her name was Amanda. He searched through his desk drawers and found the card which read "Amanda King, – Psychic Clairvoyant, South London" and her phone number.

Vince's parents had asked to speak to Detective Chief Inspector David Holroyd. They, too, were concerned about the lack of progress. It had been five days since Vince's murder and no-one knew where his female assailant was.

They had faith in the justice system but wanted to discuss with Holroyd any other possible way to move the investigation along.

Ray was asked by Holroyd to attend the meeting. He was in his boss's office when a police officer announced Vince's parents.

Jim and Margaret O'Shaunessy slowly walked into David Holroyd's office. Jim held his wife by the waist as she was leaning into him, her eyes red raw, her face haggard as if she had not slept for days, head down, unable to carry such an intolerable burden.

Ray stood very still, in total shock. There, in front of him, was the waitress that he had met some 20 years ago. Despite the grief oozing from her, she had not changed much. She did not recognize Ray at first but he knew it was her. The same eyes, the same red hair, the same pretty face, albeit 20 years older. And there was no mistaking her name "Margaret".

David Holroyd introduced Ray to Vince's parents. Margaret visibly paled as she shook hands with Ray, finally recognising him. She was already shaken by the murder of her son and this unexpected apparition from the past took her by surprise.

However she managed to shake off unwanted memories of her encounter with Ray, and composed herself enough to greet him. The Detective Chief Inspector was clueless as to what was happening and was looking from Ray to Margaret O' Shaunessy with a puzzled expression. She explained to him that she had known Ray briefly when he was a police officer and did not elaborate further.

After this initial contretemps, David Holroyd briefed the O'Shaunessy couple on his decision to engage a psychic to hopefully gain some valuable insight into Vince's murderer. This decision was well received by Vince's parents. They knew that psychics were sometimes frowned upon and dubbed con artists, but they had watched several documentaries on the power of psychics plus they had also heard of the harrowing case of the murdered little girl last year.

They knew that the only reason the murderer was behind bars was due to the psychic who had given the police vital information which had then led to the murderer being arrested and him serving a life sentence in Wandsworth prison .

Suddenly amongst all the sadness and upset, a glimmer of hope shone in Margaret's heart, somewhat appeasing her sorrow and her broken heart. She so wanted her son's killer to be caught. She missed him dreadfully already and was not sure how to go on living without him.

Although he had left home at a young age, and behaved in a silly way for a few years like most adolescents, they were close and Vince had visited her regularly. When he had started earning good money he had even sent some to her to "Buy yourself something nice, Mum. You deserve it, you are the best". He had insisted.

She knew that some of her friends sniggered behind her back about Vince being a "gigolo". She frankly did not give a damn. Margaret had always been proud of him, and of the fact that he had found something to do that he liked. She was relieved too that his "occupation" gave him a better standard of living than he had had to contend with up to recently. Plus he was so handsome, how can women not like him?

These thoughts made her heart ache even more. She truly felt that her life had no purpose now. She would never see him, breathe his smell, touch his face or hold him again, nor will she ever hold his future children.

He would never again arrive at her house riding his bike. There would be many sad Christmases and birthdays without him and the thought of those were almost too much to bear. The sense of loss was overwhelming. She felt like she had lost a limb, a big part of her body aching from the loss of her son, feeling his presence throughout her heart and soul, yet knowing that he had been suddenly cut off from her life. The devastation caused by the brutal and sudden ending of his young life, was keeping her, and Jim, awake night after night.

He had been her life, born out of wedlock, but nevertheless her precious little son. Then Jim had married her and treated Vince like his son. She would be forever grateful to have found such a kind man and such a good father. It was a shame that, after complications at Vince's birth, she had not been able to give Jim another child. Vince had remained her only child and her life.

CHAPTER 6

Amanda had just come back from holiday in the Lake District and was feeling more relaxed than when she had left. She had spent a week with her family and going "back home" always made her feel better. Her mum would fuss over her and she would enjoy silly conversation with her siblings, reminiscing about their childhood.

Nevertheless, she had decided to head on back south to return home in order to avoid the Halloween preparations which would be underway for her little niece. She had not wanted to partake in the traditional "trick or treat" activities and preferred to leave than to disappoint her niece by not joining her to go around the neighbourhood that evening.

Amanda was pretty, petite, had a cute round face, sported shoulder-length shiny brown hair, with a normally vivacious personality which still showed occasionally.

People were fond of telling her that she was the spitting image of the Sixties singer Lulu, which did not please her. Plus Lulu had red hair and hers was brown but still, in her opinion, the annoying comparison was made far too frequently!

The last couple of years had been difficult for Amanda. She had been doing some work with the police in London to locate missing persons and last summer she had helped solve a vicious and harrowing murder.

Amanda had known from an early age that she had a gift of seeing things, just like a movie playing in her mind. It had been very disturbing, especially as a young child, as she did not always understand what the images meant. With her mother's help, she had realised that she had psychic abilities and that it was possible for her to tune into events by getting a clear vision of them. Her mother, herself possessing psychic abilities, had helped her develop her intuition and had taught her how to interpret the images accurately.

She had learnt over the years to just accept her gift and now, in her early thirties she was comfortable using her intuition to help find missing persons and to provide personal readings to people.

She had never thought that her gift would give her such a successful new career, but after solving the young girl's murder last year, she had become very popular and sought-after. As the saying goes, every cloud has a silver lining.

Except that the lining of one particular cloud had not been silver but very black in the summer of last year and now her career was on the up.

She let herself into her small flat in Crystal Palace. Her answering machine was bleeping furiously, reminding her that she was back in the land of work and responsibilities. She never took her mobile phone with her when she went on holiday to her family. Her mind needed a break from the demands of her job, so cutting herself off and just chilling with her mother and siblings was the most beneficial way she had found to recharge her batteries and to regain some normality.

She pressed the button on the machine and listened to the numerous messages, mostly left by eager clients asking her for a reading. However one message caught her attention. It was from a Ray Stevens, from Croydon Police Station asking her to ring him back urgently. She knew she had to call him back but her intuition was telling her to be careful. She was not sure why, so she assumed it was because of the upset she had felt after last year's harrowing experience. She was obviously very happy to have helped catch the killer but it had left her shaky for some months because of the brutality of the attack.

Not only that, but the young girl had only been eight years old...

She unpacked and made herself a cup of tea before she tried and call Ray Stevens. He was on the phone but she was told that the Detective Inspector would ring her back shortly. She relaxed back on the settee, thinking that her intuition was sending her some strange signals. She had felt uneasy since she heard the message from Ray Stevens and, as yet, had not worked out why. Maybe when she finally spoke to him it would become clear.

Ray rang her back fifteen minutes later. He introduced himself as Detective Inspector Ray Stevens and informed her that he was in charge of an investigation into the murder of a young man and that his superior would be very grateful for her assistance. The investigation had stalled for the moment and they needed more information linked to the identity and whereabouts of the murderer if possible. He told her that the suspect, a woman who had been with the victim, had remained untraceable to date.

Amanda listened carefully, although she found Ray's slightly hoarse voice irritating, and did not understand why she was reacting like this to a man she did not know. He was merely asking her help. What was wrong with her? She was not usually so quick to be rankled by someone.

"Bummer, I've just come back from holiday and frankly I didn't fancy being part of a police investigation so soon".

She felt a bit annoyed at the thought of being thrown into a murder case after having had such a nice relaxing break. But bills had to be paid so she would use her gift to assist Ray Stevens and his colleagues. She agreed to come to the police station the following morning. She knew that, if they had bothered to ring her, there must be a certain urgency to this case. Amanda asked Ray to ensure that she would be given a picture of the victim and something of his, preferably that he had with him when he died. Ray thought about the wallet and one of the recent pictures they had been provided by Vince's parents. In case she also needed one, Ray had prepared a picture of the victim after his strangulation at the scene of the crime.

When Amanda arrived at Croydon Police Station the following morning, she was shown into the office of Detective Chief Inspector David Holroyd. He introduced himself and introduced Ray as the chief investigating officer in Vince's murder.

Amanda shook hands with both men but felt a shudder when touching Ray's hand. She stared at him, straight in the eyes, hoping to understand why she was reacting this way.

There is a saying that eyes are the mirror of the soul, and what she saw in Ray Stevens' eyes was disturbing. In his eyes, there was such loneliness, despair, unhappiness and something else she had not worked out yet. Amanda was a bit guarded but nevertheless decided to listen to what the two detectives wanted from her.

David Holroyd explained the circumstances of Vince's murder five days ago and the fact that he had been with a woman, supposedly called Vanessa but that, as yet, there had been no trace of her. He confirmed that they would be grateful for her assistance. Amanda explained that the way she worked as a clairvoyant was to tune into an object of the missing or deceased person to gain some visual information about the victim and how they met their death.

Unlike psychic mediums who received messages directly from the deceased victim or from other spirits, she would not hear from Vince, she would more likely get a vision of either the killer or get a sense of the event of that night in more detail.

She mentioned to them that, in the case of the murdered young girl, when touching her doll, and holding a picture of her, she had had a vision of where exactly her body was and had perceived the presence of a man by her side. Acting on this information, the police had quickly gone to the location, found the girl's body and successfully arrested the suspect.

"However", added Amanda," the police are the ones who solve crimes, I certainly do not. I can give your officers new clues, direction or guidance, but ultimately your team, Detective Chief Inspector, will be solving the murder".

Amanda sensed that something was disturbing Ray. He was quiet during his boss's briefing but her senses, already on the alert, were picking up warning signals. She did not know as yet if it was a personal thing or linked to the murder but, as always, Amanda trusted her intuition so she knew she would soon understand why there was uneasiness around Ray.

She asked for a quiet room to sit in to connect with the picture of Vince and hold an object of his. She also took a picture of Vince's body at the scene of the crime. She had requested it be placed in an envelope as she preferred not to use it unless she did not pick up anything significant from the other objects. She would then let them know what she saw. Ray showed Amanda to a room and left her to it. Whilst closing the door, Ray lingered and glanced back at Amanda. She was trying to remain calm and averted her gaze from his questioning stare.

Amanda centred herself, took some deep breaths and looked into Vince's eyes on the picture in front of her. At first all she felt was a strong feeling of confusion. She did not know why but she was unable to connect with him on that night. She recentered herself, calming her mind to get rid of the confustion she felt and then tried again.

This time, she held the wallet and, as if through his eyes, she saw a woman in the hotel room with Vince, thus confirming what she had been told. She suddenly experienced tremendous revulsion and nausea. Then, in a flash, a picture came to her mind. A woman's face. Her eyes. She had to really focus for the picture to be clear in her mind. No, there was no mistaking those eyes! The same eyes and the same stare she had noticed a short while ago. Here in the police station... The woman's eyes were the eyes that had disturbed and unsettled her earlier. Ray Stevens' eyes!

For a moment, she did not know what to think, she felt a mixture of fear, apprehension, repulsion and, in all honesty, intense confusion. The murder was supposed to have been carried out by a woman. Perhaps, Ray had an identical female twin? She was not sure if her intuition was letting her down on this case or if there was more to the murder than met the eyes.

Was she mistaken about the identity of the murderer? She had to be absolutely sure. There was no possible margin of error. To bring the murderer to justice, she had to be one hundred percent sure.

Amanda was feeling under pressure and she had to calm herself down for a while before she tried to get a vision again.

This time, she took out the picture of Vince's body on the bed. Her whole being shuddered as, all of a sudden, Vince was holding a woman. She saw him naked and her partly undressed. Through Vince's eyes she was staring at the woman's groin. In her head, she felt Vince utter the words "man" and "freak".

This was so unexpected that, at first, she thought she had got it wrong. It was unlikely Ray had a twin sister. But Vince had shouted "man"

It must mean that Vanessa was indeed a man, In this case, did it put Ray in the hotel room that night with Vince, dressed as a woman?

She trusted her instinct and intuition, but her logical mind was questioning the validity of her visions. The whole thing did not make sense. Ray Stevens was a detective on the case, maybe she had got it wrong. How strange for him to be investigating a murder he had committed, to be perfectly detached, almost cold and to act as if nothing had happened?

What was she to do now? Both David Holroyd and Ray were waiting for her to tell them what information she had perceived. What a dilemma as well as a difficult, and possibly dangerous, position to be in.

After all, not only had the man killed in cold blood, but he was acting as if nothing was wrong. If she denounced him, would he come after her? Would it be wiser for her to stay quiet or pretend that she saw a woman?

All these thoughts crossed her mind briefly but she knew that her spiritual nature and integrity as a human being, and as a psychic, would not allow her to let Ray get away with murder.

After all, he had killed a young man and should be punished. She would simply have to be very careful how she would impart the information to the police. More than ever she believed about justice being done.

She came out of the room and went to David's office as directed. The Detective Chief Inspector was sitting at his desk and Ray Stevens was not in the room. She hesitated, should she mention something to him now or think about it a bit more, then agree the best course of action? Before she had a chance to make up her mind, David Holroyd picked up the phone and asked Ray to join them.

"Oh well, I guess that answers my question", thought Amanda. "Now what am I going to tell them"?

David invited her to sit and they waited for Ray to enter the office. She had to think very fast. She had already thought that she should divert the investigation from a search for a woman to searching for a man.

That the killer they needed to catch was, in fact, a man who liked to go out dressed as a woman. She knew there and then what she would tell them both.

CHAPTER 7

Ray's shirt collar suddenly felt like a size too small, almost strangling him. He kept running his finger around the collar and pulling at it but this brought him no relief. He was agonising over what Amanda might discover, whilst at the same time, being impatient and eager to know what she will say. Being part of the murder investigation team, he had had to go along with Holroyd's suggestion to employ a psychic to assist in the investigation, but he had been very suspicious of the way Amanda had peered into his eyes.

He was well aware that a lot of people thought the police were wasting resources by employing psychics. Sometimes, the information given would in fact divert resources from the investigation, especially because all information received as part of an investigation had to be checked out before being classified as false or as a prank. Unfortunately some psychics had tried to make some money by working with the police and had reeled out a whole bunch of useless information.

Equally, some genuine psychics had come up with real evidence which led to solving cases.

Somewhere, in a corner of his mind, he hung on to the hope that the psychic would perceive that a woman had committed the murder, leaving him off the hook.

Ray Stevens had followed the news of the murdered girl last year, so he knew that Amanda was a credible psychic. Due to the unusual circumstances of the case, it had made headlines for days, until the murderer had final been arrested, all on the strength of Amanda's vision. Suddenly he was delaying going into the boss's office to hear what she would relate to them both.

He knew what had happened that night, a few days ago. Being honest with himself, he had to admit that he was struggling to keep a lid on his own emotions and, more than ever, with keeping Vanessa under control. It was hard to make her understand that she needed to keep a very low profile from now on, as the police thought that the murderer was a woman.

It took all his might to show up to work day after day and pretend nothing had happened. It was wearing him down, affecting his concentration and his sleep. Flashes of the night of the murder disturbed his nocturnal rest.

The inner conflict between Ray and Vanessa had never been as raging and as challenging as it was at this present moment. Apart from a rough patch in late teens, they had cohabited in relative harmony for many years now.

"A bit like an old married couple" thought Ray, with a faint smile on his lips. Killing Vince had been a huge mistake though and Vanessa should not reappear in the near future, if ever.

Ray knew that, on that fateful night, Vanessa had managed to pull herself together. Using her top, she had thoroughly wiped every surface in the hotel room where she had potentially left some fingerprints. She had searched around for Vince's phone but did not find it. Having used an old Nokia and a pay-as-you go sim card to call him, she knew that her phone would be untraceable even if the police found her number in Vince's mobile, so she did not waste more time on the elusive phone.

There had been a degree of complacency in Vanessa's actions. She knew that, when the time came, the police would not find the woman who was with Vince that night. So she had not felt that she should be too careful. She had not spotted CCTV cameras in the corridors.

In fact, her professional instinct had told her that the security in the hotel was not up to scratch. The décor, although modern, was cheap so she suspected the owner would not have invested money in expensive surveillance technology. After all, most guests in this hotel were couples like her and Vince, there just for the night. It was quantity versus quality…

Just after two o'clock in the morning, she had managed to leave the hotel unrecognised. She had removed her heavy make-up, her blonde wig and her women's clothes and donned the bath robe from the hotel. She had found a large laundry bag at the bottom of the wardrobe in the room. She had hastily placed in it, her clothes, her handbag and anything else incriminating she needed removed from the room and took it with her.

Vanessa, dressed as a man, left through the fire exit. Luckily, the door had not been alarmed so she had just pushed it and found herself in an alleyway at the side of the hotel. She wore only the bathrobe over her underwear and she had to hold it closed as the belt was tied around Vince's hands. On her feet she had the court shoes she normally wore. The night was inky dark, the air quite chilly now but, at least, it was still dry.

She had thanked the Lord that it was so early in the morning and that she had not come across anyone. She would have been hard pressed to explain her appearance, her outfit and the bag she was carrying.

Although, even if she had met someone, London, and its suburbs such as Forest Hill, was such a tolerant city that maybe no-one would bat an eyelid at a rather strange man, a bit dishevelled, in a bathrobe, carrying a large laundry bag with the name of a local hotel on it. If the situation had not been extremely serious and tragic, it would have been funny!

Ray recalled how Vanessa had managed the forty five minutes' walk to her place. How she did not come across anybody, he will never know, but she had thanked her lucky star that night. As soon as she had got home, she had showered and gone to bed.

As he had fallen asleep in the early hours of the morning, Ray had had the fleeting thought that Vanessa was getting out of hand and that he would have to get rid of this alter-ego he had created. He had warned her many times to check her temper but she took no notice. Somehow this was a feeling of déjà-vu which unsettled him.

He did not want to revisit the scene that had just popped into his head out of the blue. Now was definitely not the time to dwell on the uninvited memory which pushed its way into his consciousness. Right now he needed to sleep.

"I will think about it on my way to the station in the morning", he thought. "God - I hope Friday won't be too busy. Mind you, I guess it's unlikely. There's a few of them sick with that tummy bug doing the rounds. With everything else going on right now, this is the last thing I need." were his last conscious thoughts before he drifted into a fitful sleep.

When he had arrived at work that Friday, the chief had informed him that he was to go and investigate the murder of a young man. Ray had thought he was going to have a heart attack. His limbs had weighed a ton almost devoid of life. Fingers of fear had suddenly gripped his guts, giving him spasms and cramping pains. He had realised he was shit-scared. He hoped that the chief would not notice his reaction.

Of course, he had known that the murder would have been reported, that he would hear about it, maybe even be part of the investigation team.

He had not, however, imagined that he would be the main investigating officer into Vince's murder.

Oh the irony of it! If it was not for the stupid stomach bug, he would not be in this weird predicament. It required a herculean strength of character for Ray not to crumble completely.

CHAPTER 8

Now he had to face the psychic, and his boss, and hear whether she had guessed the identity of the murderer. Ray entered David Holroyd's office, not engaging with Amanda. She was sitting with her back to him anyway, her facial expression hidden from him. Ray sat down in the chair next to hers, both facing David.

Amanda said: "I have some important news ".

Ray's heart was beating super-fast, he even felt the blood throbbing at his temples, a sign that his blood pressure had just shot up. Was he about to be found out? He desperately forced himself not to show any emotion, neither on his face nor through his body language. He was good at controlling himself, he had had years of practice, but this was a challenge he had never imagined he would have to contend with, never in a million years.

"Damn you Vanessa" he swore in his head, dreading what Amanda was about to reveal.

"I did see something earlier, a vision. Through Vince's eyes I saw a woman, and felt Vince recoil in disgust after gawping at her genitals. I felt the word "man" and "freak" come to my mind. I'm sorry, I did not make out her face as Vince was not focussing on it at that point.

Detective Chief Inspector, I think that your investigation should concentrate on a man dressed as Vanessa that night. Not on a real woman as you thought".

Amanda sensed the palpable relief course through Ray's body as she imparted her information.

"This is quite a new development" commented Holroyd, whilst waving Ray towards the door.

"Ray, please go and brief the troops. Amanda and I will join you shortly to give them all a few more details. I just want a word with her".

Well, this was certainly not to Ray's liking. He did what he was told, went to the incident room, whilst wondering why the boss wanted to speak to Amanda without him being present? Had he guessed something was amiss in Amanda's statement to them?

Either he was being paranoid or suffering from a guilty conscience. Maybe they had to fill in all the administrative papers relating to her helping with the investigation? Who knows? But his mind was not at peace and he wondered what was being talked about in Holroyd's office right now.

The minute the door closed on Ray, Amanda got up and approached David's desk, and in a quiet voice added:

"Detective Chief Inspector, there is something really vital you need to know. I have not told you everything I saw from the murder. It is to do with Ray Stevens.

I cannot quite explain it, but I did catch a glimpse of the woman's eyes as she was looking at Vince when he was pulling away from her. I recognized Ray Stevens' eyes, only full of anger even rage. She had the same stare as I had just glimpsed when I met him in your office. Unless he has a twin sister then my guess is that Ray is Vanessa, dressed as a woman".

She was feeling stronger and stronger vibes that her intuition was correct and that Ray was the murderer. How the police were going to prove it was another matter, not her concern really as she had done what she had been commissioned to do. She may be a "psychic detective" but the onus was not on her to prove Ray's guilt. She had done her bit.

Holroyd was taken aback by the unexpected news. He had invited her to stay behind specifically because he had sensed her hesitation at recounting what her vision revealed to her. He had wondered if there was something she was reluctant to divulge in front of Ray. So he had suggested the meeting carried on without him. Well he was not disappointed.

Indeed she had some more details to reveal to him. And to say he was shocked would be an understatement. His mind was reeling with the news and it got him thinking about his colleague:

"Ray Stevens? Really? How is it possible for him to be involved in a murder? He has been a detective for 20 years. Why would he commit a crime? What did he have to do with Vanessa?" he muttered under his breath.

David had had a few occasions to share a beer with Ray after successful cases were solved, and he had never talked about a girlfriend or a wife admittedly, but him dressing as a woman? It appeared a bit far-fetched. But who was he to question his officers' sexual tendencies or unusual habits?

On top of his puzzlement about Ray's involvement in the murder, David felt the pressure of making certain that the information he had just received was correct.

Had Amanda's vision been accurate? Was she mistaken in anyway? He was aware of her excellent reputation but he had never worked with her before. Was she trustworthy?

He had to take on board the information she imparted of course, that was obvious, but this would open a monumental can of worms. He had to ensure that there was absolutely no possibility that the psychic had been mistaken and had accused the wrong person. There were enough doubters out there, so he would not give them more ammunition against the police force's use of psychic help.

Meanwhile, Amanda had detected David Holroyd's struggle with her revelation, so she waited patiently until he composed himself, and listened to what he had to say. Still pensive, he, finally glanced at her and actually expressed what she was feeling at this precise moment:

"It will all have to come out now though" he exclaimed, "If Ray is indeed Vanessa, we need to arrest him and get a confession from him. From what you have learnt so far about Ray, Amanda, how do you think we can prove that Ray is Vanessa and get him to admit that he is the killer?"

Amanda had been thinking that Ray was decidedly twitchy and fearful of any revelation. The fact that she had announced that she knew Vanessa was a man, but had been unable to identify her face, was a big relief to him and he probably assumed he had got away with murder, literally.

"What would prompt Ray to confess?" she wondered, aware that she was probably getting dragged into something a bit beyond her. "It would have to be some form of trap with Ray being unaware he was being watched or heard. My goodness, why am I playing the detective, imagining how I would catch the killer? A minute ago I was convinced my job was done."

However the Detective Chief Inspector had raised a pertinent question and this had stirred her interest. Together they would have to come up with a plan but, for the moment, David Holroyd urged Amanda to join him to give Ray's investigation team more details of the new possible suspect.

They agreed to meet the following morning in a neutral place so as not to arouse Ray's suspicion. By then David would have formulated a plan and will discuss it with Amanda.

After much reflection, that same evening, the Detective Chief Inspector concluded that the surest, but most challenging, way to get Ray to confess was to once more resort to Amanda's services. This time, it would be to let Ray know, from the horse's mouth, that she had identified him that night as the killer even though he was dressed as Vanessa.

David Holroyd decided not to tell his colleagues about the trap to be laid because what he planned on doing was not strictly legal. He was involving a civilian and this is one of the worst risks for a detective to take. The likelihood was that Ray might hurt Amanda, but every reasonable step would be taken to minimize any potential risk during her encounter with Ray. He would be following her to ensure her safety. If the situation got out of hand, he would unfortunately have to resort to calling for back-up. But, he had a weapon of choice which might just do the trick to ensure that Ray did not harm Amanda.

They had to give it a shot, having no alternative strategy to get Ray to confess. Even if Ray was arrested and interrogated, he was unlikely to admit to Vince's murder. He was well acquainted with the legal system and with police procedures.

By erasing any trace of his presence in the hotel room that night, and with no hard evidence due to lack of CCTV footage, he had ensured that, without his confession, the case against him would be very thin and would not hold up in court.

"Desperate times call for desperate measures" uttered David to himself, maybe to reassure himself that what he was planning was appropriate and that he would get the confession he was seeking.

"Horses for courses" he thought.

David had always been fond of idioms, usually finding the correct one to justify dubious actions to himself when he was having even the slightest doubt about them.

Today he felt that those two more than justified the risky side of the plan which had formed in his head.

Tomorrow he would meet Amanda in a small café near her home to discuss the plan with her, hoping that the risk involved would not put her off. He desperately needed her help to get some sort of confession from Ray. "Fingers crossed"!

CHAPTER 9

The afternoon after Amanda's visit and revelations at the police station, she called Ray. It surprised him to say the least. Little did she know how he had been mulling over her disclosure as well as wondering about the content of her discussion with Holroyd when he was out of earshot.

On hearing her voice so unexpectedly, Ray felt shivers down his spine, a feeling of gloom cloaking him. He was unsure what to expect. She came straight to the point.

"Detective Inspector? Good afternoon. Can you meet me tomorrow evening at Joanna's restaurant? It is near where I live in Crystal Palace? I have some information that will interest you. Seven o'clock okay?"

Ray was momentarily taken aback by the abruptness of her request. The implications of her attitude were not lost on him and he was apprehensive about hearing what she planned to discuss with him. Nevertheless he agreed to meet her at Joanna's.

Earlier that day, when David had highlighted his plan to Amanda, the venue had popped into her head.

She had suggested it to David who agreed. It was ideal for the meeting with Ray. She had been in the restaurant a few times with friends. It was nice, easily accessible, and often quite busy. Better still, the layout of the tables afforded diners some privacy, in case of awkward conversations. The alleyway to the side would provide a hiding spot for David's car and his listening equipment, as he laid in wait in case Ray attempted to harm Amanda.

The bait had been dangled at the end of the rod, and the fish had just taken a bite: Ray had agreed to meet her. David insisted she should wear a covert listening device (well a bug in short) under her clothes in case Ray confessed to the murder or let slip anything incriminating. It would allow him to listen in on the conversation and intervene if it emerged she was in any danger.

Holroyd wculd get the necessary equipment without involving his colleagues. Good job there was some leeway in being a Detective Chief Inspector. He was able to sign out a listening device without having to raise too much paperwork, therefore avoiding unnecessary probing questions.

Despite both parties having agreed to meet at seven o'clock, two hours before the meeting, Amanda received a call from Ray changing the time and venue. She asked him why.

She wondered if he was suspicious that this was a trap. He answered tersely that, as she well knew, he was working on a murder case so he was unable to spare more than one hour to meet her and that included the journey time from Croydon. He had to cover for some of his team members.

"Right now I can only meet you briefly. Meet me at six o'clock in Crystal Palace Park, the entrance on Anerley Hill. It's not too far from Joanna's anyway".

Before Amanda had a chance to confirm it was ok, Ray had put the phone down. This action unsettled Amanda and her mind was churning over this new development. Would she have time to warn David Holroyd of the changes to their plan? She had to contact him urgently for him to get the small radio transmitter rigged up and then get herself ready to meet Ray, all within the hour.

"Let's hope David has the stuff ready for me to wear and he can fit it on time".

She was reluctant to meet Ray in the designated venue as she knew it was a fairly deserted part of the park.

If she remembered well, it would be closing shortly after six o'clock anyway. She was grateful that someone would be listening in on their exchange and watching her back.

Still, she was now on the verge of panicking, so she forced herself to calm down and breathed deeply, all the while realising the importance of the meeting. It was vital she remained calm, not only to stay safe, but also to secure a confession from Ray.

David arrived within twenty five minutes, fitted the small bug to her t-shirt under a loose jumper and explained to her how to position herself so that Ray's voice would be picked up clearly. Apprehensive but determined to succeed, Amanda got into her car to drive to Crystal Palace Park, only ten minutes from her flat. Holroyd had followed her and parked a short distance from the entrance where Amanda was due to meet Ray. Even though the range of the bug was about 300 metres, both of them hoped that the meeting with Ray would take place near the entrance and not further inside the park. To cover this eventuality, David would follow her at a safe distance.

Amanda had been waiting for five minutes when Ray arrived. Luckily, he directed her to a bench nearby, alongside the main path. Only a few people were walking through the park, and she noticed a lone jogger. It made her feel safer knowing there were people around. Without wasting time, Ray, sitting next to Amanda, asked her what it was all about.

"I am not sure why you wanted to meet me but I am in a hurry so why don't you tell me what this meeting is about? Then we can each get on with our own business".

Refusing to be intimidated by his curt manners, she stared at him straight in the eyes and retorted:

"Ok, as you wish. During the meeting in Holroyd's office yesterday, I didn't tell the whole truth about what I saw about the night of Vince's murder.

Ray, I saw your eyes looking back at Vince, I saw the rage in them when Vince pushed you away. You were dressed as Vanessa but I know that YOU are the one who strangled Vince. I saw all of this yesterday Ray, but I have not told Holroyd yet".

Stunned and rankled, Ray nonetheless was fighting a hard battle inside to appear unaffected by her accusations. He had to deflect her, show her she was wrong and that she had no proof whatsoever. Ray suddenly got up from the bench, towered over her and he berated her sarcastically:

"Amanda, you disappoint me. Is that the best you can do? Okay. You state you saw me in your vision that night. How can you prove I killed Vince? Maybe I was there as Vanessa, but someone else might have entered the room and killed him? Have you thought of that? Even if what you say is true, how will you prove it so it stands up in court? What exactly do you want to achieve with this meeting? Blackmail? More to the point, what the hell do you want me to do about your "revelation", Amanda? Do you want my congratulations?"

Even though Ray was sarcastic and bordering on rude, Amanda knew she had him rattled and scared. She almost heard the rapid gush of the blood running too fast through his veins, throbbing visibly on Ray's temples. His blood pressure was rising and it was visible to her naked eye. She felt she had to nudge him into anger to make him lose control thus revealing more than he intended.

She had to call on Vanessa's feelings as Ray had been so good at controlling his own for many, many years.

She taunted her:" Vanessa, tell me, how did it feel to be rejected by such a handsome man that night? Did you really imagine that Vince was interested in you, Vanessa? He was only in the room because he gets paid for screwing women like you, lonely women. You are old, you are a man and Vince was right, you are a freak. There are no two ways about it Vanessa, you will only ever be a false woman, a reject of society, a weirdo."

Ray was getting more and more agitated, clearly struggling to keep a hold on himself. Amanda saw his fists tighten by his sides, his jaws clenched very tight, making his teeth grind uncontrollably, his cheeks getting redder and redder, with an almost palpable air of desperation surrounding his entire being. He was leaning closer and closer towards her, with a menacing stance all of a sudden. She knew her words were strong and provoking but frankly to get a confession, Ray had to be provoked into showing Vanessa's murderous side. Amanda had never in her life goaded a person that way but she had to carry on. Although the entire episode was totally against her nature, her desire to have justice being served was giving her the strength to taunt Vanessa further. Out of the blue, the picture of last year's murdered little girl popped in her mind which instantly raised her anger level.

She egged Ray on:

"Come on Ray, I know the truth. I saw it clearly. You know the truth too. Do the decent thing, give yourself up. Own up to what you did, show that you are a decent human being, not this crazy demented bitch who killed an innocent man because she is a psycho and a freak!"

In this very instant, as soon as she had uttered "freak", she knew Ray had lost it, he had gone and in his place stood Vanessa. She had firmly squashed Ray.

She jumped forward, snorting like a bull, arms outstretched in front of her, hands flapping, trying to grab Amanda's neck ready to strangle her.

Her face was barely human, distorted by a tsunami of rage and hatred, eyes red, mouth spitting. Amanda was petrified. Her instinct told her to move sideways to avoid being grabbed by the neck and to unbalance Vanessa. Irrational rage fuelled

Vanessa, making her reactive and impulsive, not able to think about her next action, just letting her anger rule her body. On the other hand Amanda had the advantage of logic and clarity.

She lunged at Vanessa and grabbed both her wrists. As her left hand was holding the watch on Vanessa's right wrist, something unexpected and very weird happened.

CHAPTER 10

Amanda peered deeply in Vanessa's eyes still holding the watch and experienced a sudden crystal-clear vision. In a split second she saw a younger Vanessa, long blond wig askew, her top open and torn, her skirt half hanging around her waist, crying. Then followed a vision of a skinny, young man, wearing nothing more than a t-shirt, his underwear bunched up around his ankles, shuffling backwards along a short corridor, all the while begging Vanessa for mercy. He was visibly shaking, doing everything in his power to escape the wrath of a demented, menacing, hysterical Vanessa. She remained totally unmoved by his plea, eyes lit up, a malicious smile on her face, advancing further and further forward towards him, into the deserted hallway leading to the main staircase. The young man, snivelling away, his legs wet from peeing on himself like a scared baby, still pleading, had reached the end of the hallway.

Out of the corner of his eye, he had caught a glimpse of the impressive ancient white stone staircase, the pride and joy of the university, looming behind him. Vanessa had viciously pushed him with all her strength, down the staircase.

He had stumbled, screamed and tried to hold onto something to break his fall. Unluckily for him, the mixture of the adrenaline from the fear he was experiencing, and the heavy dose of gin and vodka he had ingested until the early hours of the morning, had slowed his reflexes down.

In his befuddled mind, fogged up by fear and booze, his last thoughts had been:

"What the hell, who's this crazy fucker?"

He never knew the answer as he laid on his back, very still, his legs at a strange angle, his ankles still adorned by the underwear, in a pool of blood seeping from a fatal blow at the back of his head, onto the beautiful white flagstones of the hall in Nottingham Trent University.

Amanda paled and stiffened, unable to believe the brief but startling vision. It was so fast she struggled to comprehend it had really happened. She confronted Vanessa.

"Oh my God you killed someone else before! Vince was not the only one. My goodness, what have you done? You have to give yourself up, you are crazy. Ray, listen to me, Ray".

She was shaking him by the shoulders, trying to bring Ray back to consciousness, instead of the dangerous harpy he had suddenly become.

Like a wrestler about to tackle his opponent, Vanessa raised her arms, slapped Amanda's hands away from her, then stepped closer to her, wrapping both hands around her neck and starting to squeeze. Amanda felt the painful pressure on her throat, the airway narrowing, barely letting any air reach her lungs. She felt a bone-deep cold permeate her entire body. She gasped, unable to scream, and wriggled to loosen Vanessa's grip. In a few more seconds she would pass out and die. Terrified as she was, she silently asked for help,

"David where are you? Help me, please help me".

Vanessa's face was now bright red, her deranged mind focussed on strangling Amanda.

"You stupid bitch, you think you're very clever! Yes I did kill Vince and that pathetic excuse of a man who raped me! Guess what? You'll never be able to prove it, Ray saw to that. You jumped up little psychic. Who the fuck do you think you are?"

Her rage quickly transformed her into a venom-filled, obscenity-spewing snake.

Miraculously, the pressure on Amanda's throat loosened. Her lungs coming alive again, letting air rush in.

She took a deep breath and stared at Vanessa. She saw that David had used a Taser gun to stop Vanessa from strangling her to death. Whilst being momentarily disabled by the stun gun, David had handcuffed Ray, and pushed him on the floor before calling for a patrol police car to take him to the station. To make sure all was above board and done legally, he had read him the police caution when he came to.

David knew it was lucky no passers-by had witnessed the assault. It had given him a chance to creep up behind Vanessa without being interrupted or questioned by members of the public. It had helped that she had been so focussed on killing Amanda that she had not paid attention to anything around her. The impact of the whole episode had been minimal on the public, unlike Amanda who had nearly been strangled.

Ray had not confessed to Vince's murder during his conversation with Amanda but Vanessa had been angry enough to own up to the murder. The recording may not be admissible in court anyway but David was now banking on it being only a matter of time before Ray made a formal full confession to both murders, once he was in custody at the police station.

The urgent matter foremost in his mind was to get an officer to find the name of the student who had been killed. At least they knew why Ray had killed him or rather why Vanessa had. But why be so morbid as to keep the watch though? It had obviously belonged to his victim otherwise Amanda would not have had a vision of what happened to the young man. None of this made sense to David yet, but he would get to the bottom of this.

Whilst the pair awaited the imminent arrival of a police car to take Ray back to the police station, David enquired if Amanda wanted to press charges against Ray for assaulting her. He told her that, after a thorough interrogation and further investigation, it was highly likely that Ray would be charged with two murders. So adding Grievous Bodily Harm to the other charges would not make much difference.

Shaking her head, Amanda indicated to David Holroyd that no, she would not press charges against Ray. Suddenly realising the risk she had taken and how close to dying she had been, Amanda started to tremble from head to toe. David, grateful but concerned, put his arms around her shoulders to calm her down.

"It's ok, it's over now, Amanda. You did a good job and you were very brave" he congratulated her "I am so sorry I had to put you through that ordeal but it was the only way to get Ray to confess. Thank you".

Amanda began to feel calmer. Her tensed muscles gradually relaxed and the pain in her neck and throat was subsiding. Her blood was once again warming her body and the welcome flow made her feel alive. She was so relieved that Ray had admitted to both murders and would face justice after all.

For the second time that evening, she cast her mind back to the summer of last year, wholeheartedly wishing her psychic gift had served her as well then as it had today. If only she had been aware earlier of who had taken her beautiful vibrant little Kelly, she might have prevented the paedophile who abducted her, from killing her. The picture of Kelly's abused body and the feeling of hatred towards her killer had been with her every waking moment since that fateful summer. Yes, thankfully, he was behind bars, but she would live forever with the guilt of not intuiting much earlier where Kelly was.

After that tragedy, she had no longer wanted to use her gift. She felt it had betrayed her when it mattered the most. The thought of witnessing more unnecessary deaths became unbearable to her. Added to her tragic loss, she had had to contend with the media harassing her. The newspapers had enjoyed making jokes out of the situation, despite the tragedy that had hit her. After a week or so, the sensational, distressing, revolting, gutter press headlines like "Psychic's daughter murdered; she did not see it coming…" finally stopped. The media interest was diverted to another poor victim, which then afforded her some much needed space to grieve in peace.

In time, her mother had convinced her that she should carry on using her clairvoyance gift to help catch as many criminals as possible and stop another Kelly from being viciously murdered. Her mother was wise and right as usual, although it had been, and still was, heart-breaking to wake up every morning, knowing full well she will never again hold her little girl or watch her grow up…

CHAPTER 11

Ray arrived handcuffed at the police station, accompanied by a police officer who logged in his arrest as being under suspicion of two murders. The Detective Chief Inspector would start the interrogation process as soon as feasible. The news of Ray's arrest spread like wildfire around the police station and no-one understood how this was possible. Of course they knew Ray was a bit strange, never very communicative, quite honestly, not good at relating to others at all, but a murderer? Never! He had been a cop for over twenty years, why would he kill someone? His more generously-spirited colleagues hoped that maybe he had acted in self-defence and would face lesser charges. Rumours were rife.

Some had even ventured that Ray was possibly on the spectrum of high-functioning autism. This would certainly explain his aloofness, his lack of relationships, and his difficulty in relating to his colleagues with regards to day-to-day chitchat. They did not know about Vanessa yet, so comments and rumours would be even rifer when it all came out in the next few hours. One way or another his career and his life were both in tatters and no-one had wished that for him.

Ray was taken into a custody cell awaiting to be interviewed. He had time suddenly to reflect on what had just taken place in the park and make sense of the events of the night. He had been set up by his own boss, David Holroyd, and the psychic, Amanda. He might have got away with it if bloody Vanessa had not messed up again? Will she never learn to keep quiet? Will she ever stop being angry and stop reacting aggressively every time? He guessed this was asking a lot from her. He knew the suffering she had endured for years and felt sorry for her. But she had finally messed up big time with Vince's murder.

It had been bad enough Ray covering for her after she killed Jeff Burgess at University. Luckily the fact that Jeff had not been spotted going to this room, around midnight, with a young woman, had played in Ray's favour. When the police interrogated all the alumni, he gave his version of events which satisfied the cops. He told them that he had observed Jeff go into his room with bottles of drinks the previous evening, around eleven clock.

"No doubt he was drinking heavily, Jeff liked gin and vodka. Strange combination if you ask me but then again, he is a strange guy!

Admittedly, it is freshers' week, so everyone gets quite pissed and pulls weird stunts. I suspect he had a bet with someone. How else would you explain him being bare arse with his pants around his ankles? His dare probably was to go down the stairs backwards with his pants down. I tell you, officer, I think this is an accident, an unfortunate dare gone wrong".

Ray had been quite convincing. His explanation was indeed very plausible. Plus, no-one was aware a woman had been with him that night. Even if someone had noticed her, they would never guess her identity, let alone find her. No concrete evidence of foul play had been found so the verdict from the coroner was "accidental death".

Ray had called the police pretending that he had just found a body on his way back into the hall after a night out. Shortly, after Jeff had fallen to his death, Ray had deftly removed the expensive watch from his wrist, being careful not to disturb the body. Straight away he had gone to hide the watch in his room, changed quickly back into Ray, then he waited near the body in the hall until the police arrived. Whilst waiting, he had reviewed the evening in his head, with the sole purpose of testing the version of events which best explained Jeff's death.

Of course he had to anticipate the possible discovery that Jeff's watch was missing

After thinking it through, he concluded that Jeff's parents would not yet know about the watch so they would be unlikely to report its theft to the police. He recalled Jeff had told him he had used his rent money to buy it so it was unlikely he had been bragging about acquiring such an expensive watch to his parents, or to anyone else for that matter.

In reality, it was not the value of the watch that had enticed Ray into stealing it, more the desire to have a reminder to never get into a similar situation in the future, certainly never to kill again. He was deeply shaken but as usual was able to hide his true emotions. The one feeling which sustained Ray was that Jeff had deserved what he had got. After all, Vanessa had fancied the little bastard and had spent the evening with him, drinking and having fun. Then it all got out of hand. Vanessa was never able to resist flirting and coming on to pretty men like this idiot. Problem was that, when Jeff realised she was a man, he had laughed at her, and then pinned her down and raped her. Ray knew that Jeff was bisexual anyway so clearly, he did not mind a bit of "backside action" himself.

Poor Vanessa had not intended for this to happen. It had been her first sexual encounter as Vanessa and it had become a nightmare. She was only 19 years old, a virgin and she had romantic ideas about how her first time should have gone. It had not included non-consensual sodomisation somehow. This was a long time ago, but now the memories of Jeff's death flooded Ray's mind as if it had happened yesterday. Being accused of Vince's recent murder, was bound to make him remember Jeff's too.

Ray needed to make sure Vanessa understood that he had got into trouble defending her once again and did not intend to carry on doing that forever.

Detective Chief Inspector Holroyd and the detective now in charge of Vince's murder and of Ray's arrest, were ready to start the interrogation. David had already sent a team to Ray's house to garner whatever evidence they could find to corroborate what had transpired during his conversation with Amanda.

An interview room had been set up with the necessary recording equipment. Ray had been read his rights and he had asked for a solicitor to be present.

A duty solicitor had been called and. for once, had arrived quickly, so David Holroyd was all set to unravel this baffling mystery. His colleague had been in custody for two hours. Every hour was precious, as Ray would either have to be charged or released after 36 hours. David knew that, having been arrested on suspicion of two murders, it was unlikely that Ray would be granted police bail, so from now on there would be no taste of the outside for Ray for some time, especially if they were going to charge him.

Although he did not yet understand what had pushed Ray to kill, twice, he did feel a twinge of compassion for this man he had worked with for the last ten years. He had found Ray to be a conscientious, hard-working detective, at least since he, himself, had taken over as Detective Chief Inspector. The only flaw in Ray's character, in David's opinion, was his aloofness and the uneasiness which exuded from him. The noticeable and ever-present feeling that Ray was not comfortable in his own skin often unsettled a lot of his colleagues. Sadly, Ray had never been close enough to anyone to explain his discomfort. Hence all the speculation going on within the police station right now.

CHAPTER 12

In the interview room, David Holroyd started the interrogation of the suspect:

"For the benefit of the tape please state your full name and date of birth".

"Ray Edward Stevens, 14th September 1973".

"Thank you. This interview is conducted on November 2nd 2018, starting at 22h15. Officers present are Detective Chief Inspector David Holroyd and Detective Inspector James Carter, now in charge of the investigation into the murder of Vince O'Shaunessy. Also present, at the request of the accused, is a duty solicitor, Miss Jayanti Anand.

Mr Stevens has been arrested on suspicion of the murder of Vince O'Shaunessy on the night of 25th October 2018 in London and of the murder of a student, Mr Jeff Burgess on 9th October 1992 at Nottingham Trent University. Ray, please explain to us who Vanessa is? "

David Holroyd waited with anticipation for what Ray would say, hoping that the interview would be fairly straightforward, with Ray confessing to both murders and signing a statement to that effect.

Then this statement, and any other potential evidence, would form the case filed with the Crown Prosecution Service and presented to the Crown Court for a judge to decide on Ray's fate. With a bit of luck, Ray would plead guilty so no jury would be required, the sentencing being decided by the judge in such cases. Whichever way Ray eventually pleaded, from where David stood, this whole incident was not good for the reputation of the local police station. He certainly did not want the case to drag on and on, or to be challenged by the Crown Prosecution Service.

"She is my twin sister", whispered Ray.

David was straining to hear.

"Sorry I did not hear that Ray, did you answer "she is your twin sister"? Can you repeat what you said louder for the benefit of the tape please?"

"Vanessa was my twin sister. She died when we were both 15. A few months before her death, I had started to build a sort of a house in a big tree in my parent's garden. I have always liked carpentry. I just wanted to build a den for myself to have alone time when I needed to. Although I loved Vanessa very much and we were close, I needed times by myself. I always felt a bit distant from the rest of the family.

Not from her, but from my parents and other relatives. I was not very sociable.

Anyway, I had built the base as a sort of platform but not the walls yet. One April day, we were bored, staying indoors because of the heavy rain, so we decided to play dare. I dared her to climb onto the platform of the tree house and to jump from there onto the ground. It was not that high so I saw no danger in it. Anyway, she started to climb.

It had become very slippery with the rain. As she was raising herself to get onto the platform, she lost her footing and fell backwards. Somehow she fell at such a strange angle that her neck snapped and she died. I rushed to her but she was dead. I was so shocked. I called out to my mother and she asked me what Vanessa had been doing, climbing up in the tree.

When I told her she began to blame me, telling me I should not have pushed her to climb. I was so lost I did not know why she reacted that way. Anyway we buried her and life had to go on.

Needless to say, I've felt guilty ever since. In fact after her death, I changed my mind about being a carpenter and I became a policeman. After she died, my parents refused to talk to me with any affection or even with civility.

They expected me to act as a robot, I was not allowed to show sadness or grief. Only they were. I had killed her, they reminded me constantly, and I was denied the right to show grief. I was forbidden to speak to them about either Vanessa's life or her death. They held me responsible for the accident and they made me pay for it.

I have had to control my feelings and emotions from the day Vanessa died. I was stifled by them and by the grief. I just did not know how to live without her and with the guilt.

We had been so close until she died. I think I will always remember her face when she was lying on the ground, at the bottom of the tree. Her head was at a strange angle but her face was peaceful as if asleep.

Afterwards, I became unable to cope with strong emotions. I was already a pretty closed book thanks to having been bullied at school for years just like Vanessa. Kids made fun of our clothes because my parents bought second hand uniforms not always in good condition. They often had holes in them or were frayed. They called us weirdo because we were close, some even taunted us, by proclaiming to everyone that we were lovers, so they called us freaks and sickos all the time.

It was a nightmare. None of what they accused us of was true. We just had a deep bond like most twins do. Vanessa used to get angry, swearing back at them, at times kicking a few of the kids when the teachers were not present.

I dealt with the bullying differently, by hiding how I felt and never showing they had affected me. I became good at hiding what was inside my heart and inside my head. We tried to tell our parents but they just told us to get on with it and concentrate on our school work.

So we tried to, but I had noticed Vanessa was getting angrier with the bullies and with herself. I understood her. She thought she should stand up to them but she was not strong enough".

Ray paused to catch his breath, as if lost in his story and his sorrow. His eyes filled up blurring his vision. He took a sip of water from the glass placed in front of him. Staring straight at Holroyd, almost unseeing, he carried on, his voice laden with sadness.

"I started to cross-dress as Vanessa when I was 18. I missed her so much, she was so spirited, stubborn but fun and lively. In many ways so different from me. We were very much alike physically but different temperaments.

When I started to dress as her, I felt so close to her. It was a way to give her the life which was taken from her. When I was Vanessa, I felt emotions, I expressed myself but unfortunately with every bout of becoming Vanessa, I started to feel anger just like she did. Anger against my parents, against the kids, against myself and the years have not dissipated this anger. Every birthday that passes, I remember that a part of me is missing. I can't stand my birthday. I have not celebrated it since we were both 15.

At first, I would dress as her, then go to the occasional parties in nearby towns where other teenagers did not know me well. Then my parents insisted I went to University, they wanted me gone out of the house, out of their sight, as I reminded them of the tragedy they had suffered. So I went. To alleviate the loneliness, I cross-dressed much more, not during the lectures, but in the evening. One day I met a student, Jeff Burgess, and he was interested in me, in Vanessa. This was the first time I thought about having sex with someone. Of course I was curious so I followed him to his place one night. He started to drink quite a bit as soon as we entered his room in the main hall. Then we started snogging and when he realised I was a man, he laughed, called me weirdo and he raped me".

Ray was visibly struggling when recounting the rape. He was wringing his hands together over and over, obviously distraught. David asked him if he wanted to pause for a while.

"No. Thanks. I prefer to carry on. This has been such a burden for so long that I just want to get it over and done with. I flipped. Sometimes, although we were so different, I just felt like Vanessa was not only present in the way I dressed, but I also experienced what she was feeling and I found it hard to resist or manage this anger of hers. I think it is no longer just anger, it is sheer rage and it doesn't take much to activate it. It's been so hard to resist the temptation and desire to dress as Vanessa because I feel so close to her then. But increasingly I am struggling with who she has become and the trouble she has caused me.

Vanessa flipped after the rape but it was me, Ray who killed Jeff. I was a virgin and this guy sodomised me. Imagine the humiliation and the degradation I felt. The little prick thought it was hilarious. He was bisexual so he knew what he was doing but I was shocked, in pain and so humiliated I started chasing him down the hall. When he got near the top of the stairs, I just knew what I had to do. The push was such a relief.

He was so ridiculous, bare arse, with his pants around his ankles, crying like a fucking baby. I wanted to hurt him as much as he'd hurt me by raping me. The little bastard got everything he deserved!"

"How did you manage to get away with Jeff's murder until now, Ray" puzzled David.

"I am the one who phoned the police pretending that I had just come back from a night out and found the body. The rest was easy as there was no proof that he was pushed and he was highly intoxicated. Plus on fresher's week there are always stupid students pulling stupid stunts. It was declared an accidental death. Nobody had been aware of Vanessa's presence either".

"Why keep the watch though?"

"Well why not? I needed something to remind me that I must never get in that sort of trouble again or, more to the point, that Vanessa must not get to her tipping point again. I loved my sister so much but more and more I found myself spending time as her and being consumed by her anger. If I am honest that scared me, Vanessa scared me because I didn't know how to stop her from taking over my mind.

When the urge became so strong, it was almost as if she was there, in my body, propelling me forward and making me do exactly what she wanted. I was no longer Ray, I was just Vanessa. I can't explain it."

Ray shrugged his shoulders, as if in total hopelessness.

CHAPTER 13

Frankly David and his colleague, James, were both baffled themselves by Ray's confession and this dual personality phenomenon, as they had never encountered it in their respective careers. Plus, what stunned David the most was that, here was a colleague he had worked with for ten years, and he had never noticed his dilemma, his grief and had never guessed he had another personality other than being Ray. Yes, he was a strange man and now David understood much more about Ray's inability to communicate with his peers and also the uneasiness around him. He was never really himself by all accounts, so it was possibly the duality in him which was felt by others and which unsettled people around him.

"Ok. Ray can you now describe the events leading to Vince's murder please?"

Ray looked at Jayanti, his solicitor, with enquiring eyes. She nodded as if to indicate he should go ahead and tell the detectives what happened that night.

"After the rape, it took me two years to feel confident enough to even approach a woman. I fancied a young waitress in a café across the road from the police station.

Her name was Margaret. The same Margaret who was introduced to us a few days ago as Vince's mother, as you know. After my brief encounter with her, I tried really hard to give up being Vanessa but there was always something to remind me of her not being in my life.

As Ray, I had to be good all the time or my parents would hit me, they disliked me so much after Vanessa's death that I started hating myself too.

I found that controlling all my emotions, and doing my job very well, brought me a degree of peace albeit a rather boring life. But as Vanessa, I felt alive. The only way for me to express how I felt was to be Vanessa. I had watched Vince many times riding his bike in the streets near where I lived. I'm not sure what attracted me, maybe his red hair which reminded me of Margaret's. I am not into men at all but there was something compelling about Vince.

I went a few times to the club where he worked, once dressed as Vanessa. That night I even took a picture of him pretending to take a selfie. He was working behind the bar and I felt a strong urge to take a photo. Of course, he never even noticed me. As usual he was surrounded by attractive females.

He always was. Then the next time, I went there as Ray, I learnt he had been doing male escorting for a while.

I just saw a chance to get close to him and took the risk to book him for one night and I would go as Vanessa of course. I thought it may be a bit embarrassing when he realised I was a man, but these days cross-dressing and transgender people are more accepted so I naively thought it would be ok. I had not banked on his intense reaction at all, to be honest. It took me by surprise and when he started the name calling, I saw red. I had taken an immense risk to spend the night with Vince and I deserved a bit of respect. But Vince was just like all the others who tormented me and Vanessa for years. I was not prepared to take any more abuse or rejection. I lost it. I strangled Vince and left the hotel".

"Ray Stevens, are you admitting to the murder of Vince O'Shaunessy on the night of 28th October?" James asked.

He had let David take the lead in carrying out the interview up to that point, as he knew that, compared to the experienced Detective Chief Inspector, he, James was a mere rookie.

Still it was his first murder case and he was eager to secure a confession from Ray.

"Yes, I did kill Vince O'Shaunessy on the night of 28th October but I would like to plead diminished responsibility due to mental issues. I want to ask for psychiatric assessments".

Ray had had a word with his solicitor before the interview and, after outlining his side of the murder, she had advised him to plead diminished responsibility because of his state of mind, mainly caused by the abuse he had been subjected to since he was a young child, not helped of course by his parents' accusations and emotional neglect throughout his teenage years.

"Ray, you will undertake psychiatric assessments, the results of which will determine whether you will face a charge of first degree murder for both killings, or face a charge of second degree murder of Jeff Burgess and first degree murder of Vince O'Shaunessy. In the meantime you will remain in custody here and I am requesting to keep you in custody to the maximum of 96 hours. Anything you want to add to this first interrogation, Ray? No? Interview terminated at ten past midnight".

Ray had indicated no by shaking his head so Holroyd asked the officer guarding the interview room to take the prisoner back to the custody cell. He was allowed to confer with his solicitor if he so wished.

"What a turn of events" exclaimed David, by now completely flabbergasted at Ray's confession and tale of what his life had been like for the last thirty years, since his sister died.

"It just goes to show that you never really know what goes on in other people's life" added James.

"James, please organise the paperwork to extend Ray's custody to 96 hours and request the psychiatric assessments. It would be interesting to hear what the specialists make of him. Such a terrible loss for someone quite young. Then being treated as a murderer, a pariah and ostracised by his parents. Mind you, in view of the other two murders Ray has committed, one has to wonder if he was responsible back then too. Why would the parents blame him so readily for his sister's death otherwise?

I suspect that this upbringing and his parents' attitude certainly did not help him feel comfortable in himself and it explains the isolation and lack of emotions and social skills.

Please keep all this under wrap for now, James, until we have the results of the psychiatric assessments. There are enough rumours going around, we don't need more gossip about Ray. Plus we need to wait and see what forensics find at Ray's house to corroborate his confession. That confession alone is not enough to place him as the scene of the crime so let's see what the team will come up with".

Whilst David made his way to his office, James went back to the investigation office with the tape and the statement Ray had signed. However the charges and sentencing depended on the results of the psychiatric assessments still to be carried out.

David Holroyd had not long been back in his office after interrogating Ray, when one of the officers sent to Ray's house put his head around the door and asked to speak to him.

"Come in, Peter".

"Chief, you won't believe what we found in Ray's house. The forensic team is still over there, so is the photographer. I just came to let you know what we saw in case it helped you with the interrogation. Although it seems you have already finished it".

"What did you find then?" David was rather curious and a bit apprehensive too at Peter's urgent tone of voice.

"Well, picture this, Chief! We found a spare bedroom in Ray's house, with women's clothes in a wardrobe, false breasts in a drawer also full of bras, very tight underwear and thick tights, make-up items on a dressing-table and women's shoes. In a size 9 would you believe? So this definitively confirms that Ray was dressing as Vanessa. On the wall facing the bed was a poster size picture of her at the club with Vince in the background. But get this, it was covered with lipstick marks as if the photo had been kissed a number of times. A bit sick really if you ask me… Plus around it, were a few pictures of a guy with red hair on a Harley, obviously the murder victim on his bike from what I understand…

There's another weird thing. A couple of newspapers cuttings were also stuck on the wall. There were all articles reporting the tragic death of a student at Nottingham Trent University about 25 years ago. Does this make sense to you Chief? Obviously the team is taking pictures but I wondered if the newspaper article was something you should know about as soon as possible".

"Yes indeed, good thinking! Ray did confess to having covered up the murder of a student as a freshers' week prank gone wrong. Did you find anything else in his house that links Ray/Vanessa to Vince's murder without any possible doubt?" David was asking with hope in his voice, suddenly feeling that the case might finally be coming together. He needed very concrete evidence of Ray's involvement as Vanessa in Vince's murder.

"The guys were examining the rest of the house and I am expecting a call from them so I will let you know as soon as I hear anything. I just came back to try and catch you in the interview ..." just as he was about to finish his sentence, his mobile rang.

"Hi, what have you got for me?"

Peter was listening intently to his caller and his face was showing a mixture of shock, incredulity and eventually a smug grin. He ended the call, looking at David with a smirk on his face.

"Well, well, well! You'll never guess what the team has found now." Peter was delighted to impart some obviously very important information about the team's discovery.

"At the bottom of the wardrobe, there was a big plastic laundry bag, with the name Woodman Inn on it and women's clothes as well as a bathrobe with the same hotel logo. From what I saw in the original statement, that is the name of the hotel where Vince was found murdered. A missing bathrobe was mentioned in the statement written after the initial crime scene investigation. The weirdest thing is that they found a toilet seat underneath the bed. It obviously doesn't come from Ray's house so not sure where it is from. Any idea?"

"Yes! It was wrenched from the hotel toilet by Vanessa, well Ray, and used to hit the victim. Make sure forensics check it for prints and DNA".

"No problem Chief. Will let them know straight away. You know what though? I still can't get my head round Ray being sent to investigate a crime HE committed. This is just too weird!! How can Ray act as if nothing had happened and carry on looking for a murderer who is himself? This is stuff of movies. That's not real! With due respect, the guy can't be right in his head, can he Chief?"

Peter was clearly struggling to comprehend the ins and out of the extremely bizarre circumstances of this unusual murder.

"Peter, I understand that this is not a usual crime but I would urge you not to spread any rumours or gossip about it around the station.

As you well know, Ray has been one of our colleagues for many years and like everyone else, he is presumed innocent until proven guilty. So we have to stay open-minded until we know what the charges against him will be. Is that clear, Peter?" David's tone of voice left no doubt as to the seriousness of his request.

"Now ask one of your guys still at the house to bring in the picture of Vanessa and get it reprinted to show to the concierge or anyone else in the Woodman Inn who may have noticed her that night. We need to formally place her at the scene of the crime".

Peter nodded his ascent as he left the office and went to join his team to deal with his boss's request.

Left alone in his office, David Holroyd was feeling very sad and a bit mystified about his former colleague. He remembered now that Ray had never invited anyone to his house. David had invited him, and others, at summer BBQs on several occasions but the invitation had never been reciprocated. David had put it down to Ray's lack of social graces but in fact it was most probably because Ray did not want anyone to discover his secret.

Unaware of what had been found in his house, back in his cell, Ray was drained and extremely shaken-up. Reliving the event of the past thirty years had been very unsettling and distressing. It had highlighted to him how much of his life had been spent making amends for Vanessa's death and how he had ruined his own life in the process.

He acknowledged to himself, at long last, that he had been in a state of denial for years about Vanessa's negative impact on his life. At times, he was consumed by a rage that Vanessa's death was fuelling. He had tremendous difficulty in stopping himself from regularly and sometimes unexpectedly, being taken over by Vanessa. He depended so much on this dual identity to cope with life's ups and downs, his disappointments, his loneliness, his unsuccessful life. Deep in his heart he knew that he, Ray, was the law-abiding policeman of the last 20 years. Equally when being Vanessa, he was able to express the emotions he had learnt to suppress and bury deep inside. She was the rebellious, wilder, angry side of his personality. So much so that, by embracing her raging anger, he had unwittingly killed his son and in the process ruined his career, in fact his entire life.

For decades, he had been so scared of losing her for good that he had sacrificed his life for her memory. But regardless of the realisation he came to right now, he was no more able to stop his toxic connection to Vanessa than he was able to stop breathing. She would be within him to his dying day.

CHAPTER 14

Both the family liaison officer and the police officer, John Clark, now well-known by the couple, came to announce to Vince's parents that Ray Stevens, alias Vanessa, had confessed to murdering Vince. On hearing this new development, Jim and Margaret were taken aback and Margaret suddenly fainted. The two officers were rather dumbfounded by her unexpected reaction. Was Margaret fainting because it had all got too much for her, was the news such a shock and, in which case, why? A few minutes later, Margaret came too, her face as white as a sheet, sweat pouring from her forehead to her eyebrows, yet shivering.

"She is in shock" shouted Jim. "She needs a stiff drink to bring her round. Pass us the bottle of Scotch behind you, John".

He was not sure either of the reason for such a strong reaction to the news but he knew Margaret would explain it to him when she was able to.

Margaret downed the stiff drink Jim handed her and regained a degree of composure. She got up and thanked the officers and, as they were leaving, she made a strange request.

"Please ask Detective Chief Inspector Holroyd if I would be allowed to visit the prisoner very briefly? It is very important that I speak to him urgently".

John replied "Leave it with me, I'll check if it's possible. It is out of the ordinary but of course I will speak to the boss. Ray Stevens is in custody for another 60 hours so it will have to be pretty soon. Mind you I don't suppose he will be released on police bail in the near future. I'll get back to you very soon. Goodnight for now Margaret, Jim."

Having nodded his goodbyes, he left with his colleague, wondering all the way back to the station why the mother of a murdered man was wanting to meet his suspected killer. Mind you, a few times, he had met relatives of victims who had needed to speak to the killer of their loved ones to gain some closure or peace of mind and even, at times, to let them know that they were forgiving them. Personally, if someone as much as touched a hair from either his teenage daughter, or from his little boy's head, he would swing for them. He may be a police officer, but he was a dad too and he did not relish the thought of being in Jim and Margaret's shoes right now.

John went straight to the Detective Chief Inspector who, before granting the request, sought permission from his superior.

It was not usual for a prisoner in custody to be allowed to get a visit until he was charged. But, in view of the fact that Ray had previously known Margaret, after consulting with Ray's solicitor, it had been agreed that the visit would be allowed. Margaret would talk to Ray briefly, in an interview room, at Croydon Police Station.

Of course, throughout the interview, his solicitor would be present as well as the senior investigating officer for the case and the family liaison officer to provide moral support. As Ray was awaiting a psychiatric assessment to be carried out as soon as possible, Margaret would be able to visit him the following morning.

At the agreed time, Margaret, fully composed, albeit tired, but dignified and elegant in her black coat, showed up alone at the police station and gave her name. Like in most police stations, the reception area was busy, however she was expected, so the family liaison officer came to meet her and she was shown promptly to an interview room already set up.

Both Ray's solicitor and Detective Inspector James Carter were there and, after they all sat down, Ray was brought in from the custody cell by a police officer.

He had been told that Margaret had requested to visit him and he did not know what to make of this request. Rather strange really and highly irregular but when his solicitor had asked him about it, he somehow felt that he had to agree to her visit. He was curious yet his heart was beating very fast in his chest and his breathing had gone somewhat shallow. He suddenly felt very oppressed, with an ominous feeling that something bad was going to happen.

He sat down opposite Margaret who opened her handbag and took out two pictures. One of a baby and the other of a young adult. She placed both of them on the table in front of Ray and pushed them towards him. Her face was very solemn and pale, the dark circles under her red eyes highlighted the toll the last few days had taken on for her and her family. In her sorrowful eyes, there was anger, deep sadness plus something he had glimpsed in Vince's eyes that night. Revulsion.

Ray gazed down at the pictures, feeling Margaret watching his reaction.

"Vince was your son. This is him as a baby when Jim stepped in as his dad, and that is the young man you killed! Look at them carefully, Ray. You murdered not only my son, but yours.

Even worse Ray... you, or whoever you're pretending to be, bloody Vanessa, booked him as an escort for sex. The thought of you and him makes me gag Ray! It's disgusting, it's... it's incestuous!"

Margaret nearly chocked on the word. She was so disturbed by this realisation that she was struggling to articulate her thoughts and to even speak the word which caused her tremendous distress.

"I feel like puking just imagining you lying next to my precious Vince. Why him Ray? Why not pick on someone else? Why did it have to be him? Right now I'm not sure how you are gonna live with what you did and I don't really care. I am struggling with it big time. I wish to God you rot in hell for the rest of your wasted miserable life."

Her voice faltered, strangled with emotions. She was gawping at Ray with intense loathing. Tears suddenly welled up in her eyes, momentarily clouding her vision of this man she so hated.

Under her stare, Ray felt his heart constrict. Suddenly fear, pain, disgust were squashing his chest as if a huge boulder had landed on his lungs, ribs and heart, slowly but surely crushing them.

His body drained of blood and heat. He felt terribly cold as if he had jumped into icy waters in the middle of winter. The freezing cold was gripping his heart and every cell of his being. His head was both pounding and light. His arms were dead weights hanging like useless appendages alongside his body. He was so short of breath that his mouth moved like that of a fish out of water gasping for air.

He did not utter a word just looked at Margaret with a mixture of despair and self-disgust. His mind was reeling with the realisation he was having a heart attack and with the shock of the revelation.

As he collapsed on the floor, Ray's imploring eyes turned to James Carter who had rushed towards him. Ray had never been into religion, but at this moment, he prayed for forgiveness and for his life to be taken away.

"Oh Vince, no... I didn't know, I didn't know you were my son. What have I done? Forgive me Vince. Please God just let me die ".

With James attending to Ray, the solicitor left the interview room, rushing to get a first aider whilst calling for an ambulance.

It was hardly surprising to both of them that Ray was having a heart attack. After such revelations they too felt rather shocked and shaken. It would take a very strong person not to buckle under the weight of the accusations. They both understood now why Margaret had insisted on seeing Ray as soon as she knew he was Vince's killer.

She had grasped the full impact of the brief sexual encounter which luckily had not been consummated. But at what cost! Unwittingly, by saving himself from being a victim of incest, Vince had paid a high price and instead had become a murder victim.

David Holroyd, having been informed of the suspect's heart attack, despatched a police officer in the ambulance with Ray. He was being taken to A&E at Croydon University Hospital and the officer's duty would be to guard Ray, as he was of course under arrest on suspicion of murder.

No opportunity would be given to Ray to escape in case he had faked a heart attack to avoid judgement. An officer would be staying outside the Intensive Care Unit for a while though, if Ray's condition was really as serious as David suspected.

During the commotion, Margaret had got up abruptly, impatient to leave and to never be in Ray's presence again. She had done what she came here to do. Frankly, death would be too easy a way out for him. She wanted him to be as tormented by her revelation as she was.

She rushed out, almost pushing the family liaison officer out the way. She was willing herself to ignore the unprompted memories of all those years ago coming to her mind.

When she had first met him, he had been a bit of a nerd. When they had talked whilst she served him, she had felt he was not really himself. That something was not right with his mind, that he was hiding something important which made him deeply unhappy.

There had definitely been something unsettling about him. Something strange, difficult to explain, even all those years later. Nevertheless, against her better judgment, at the end of one particularly lonely and tiring week, she had felt compelled to agree to an evening out with him.

Whenever she thought about that one and only evening together, when he had lost his virginity to her, back at his place, she felt very ill at ease and a bit nauseous. She was not even sure how she had managed to get pregnant during the hurried, unpleasant sexual encounter.

She had chosen not to tell him he had fathered Vince. She had wanted nothing to do with him and so far, she had never regretted her decision not to pursue a relationship with him.

Over the years she had, only very occasionally, wondered what had happened to him. Deep in her heart, she had wondered if she should have told him about Vince years ago.

Maybe if she had, he may not have approached him as he did and Vince might still be alive. She was going to have to live with this guilt. The decision she had been so sure was the right one years ago, was now causing her intense agony and pain.

She had never told Jim either who Vince's father was. Now she had to go home and tell this gentle, loving man about the disturbing events that had befallen their family. As if coping with Vince's murder was not challenging enough!

EPILOGUE

After a few days in the Intensive Care Unit, Ray's condition improved. He was transferred to a private room until he recovered sufficiently to go back to jail. Lying in bed, still connected to various tubes and monitors, Ray heard someone talking outside his room and his eyes followed the door as it opened.

"What the hell are you doing here?"

Completely non-plussed, Ray could not work out what was going on.

"Hello Ray! It's time for your medication" said the nurse. "A little top-up of morphine to ease the pain".

"I asked you what you're doing here, how did you get in my room?" Fear was making Ray's voice tremble and his questions sound like a whisper.

"I work here, you see. So the nice police officer guarding your room just let me in. Am only doing my job, Ray. Anyway, enough with the questions, let's just get on with giving you your med, shall we??"

The nurse approached the bed in one fast stride, reaching for the drip bag. Ray's body and hands were not responding to his efforts to grab and press the alarm button resting by his side on the bed, or even to raise his hand to stop the nurse from injecting the content of a syringe into his drip bag.

His fear was so intense that his voice was suddenly silent, his throat now refusing to produce any sound. His confused mind was still unable to comprehend what was happening. He heard a bitter laugh and words that chilled him right to the core of him.

"So long Ray. Go to hell you bastard. You took Vince's life & destroyed his future. I'll never forgive you and I sure can't bear the thought of you alive, in jail, whilst Vince is dead. You are rotten Ray, a waste of space, a sicko. I say good riddance".

Watching the overdose of the toxic, lethal drug working its effect on Ray, then witnessing his last breath, Jim felt grateful for his job as a male nurse which he had always enjoyed. Even more so because today, justice of all justice, it had just given him a chance to avenge the murder of his beloved son, Vince. He had willingly risked his future for this chance.

Despite this small victory though, a sad expression adorned his face as he walked out of the room, past the police officer and out of Croydon University Hospital.

Dear Reader,

Thank you for choosing my book and I hope you enjoyed the story.

Your feedback is welcome, so please feel free to leave a comment on my Facebook page, Andrée Roby@RegineDem.

Until the next book, all the best.

Andrée x

Lightning Source UK Ltd.
Milton Keynes UK
UKHW041034090219
337018UK00001B/104/P